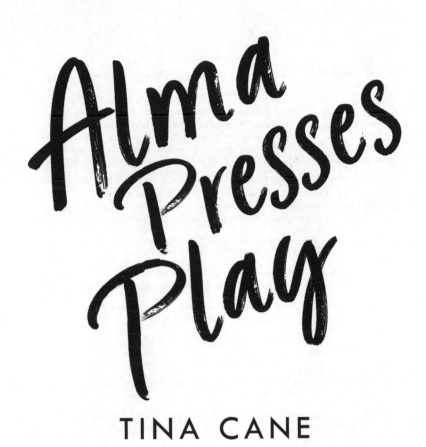

Alma Presses Play

TINA CANE

MAKE ME A WORLD

New York

MAKE ME A WORLD is an imprint dedicated to exploring the vast possibilities of contemporary childhood. We strive to imagine a universe in which no young person is invisible, in which no kid's story is erased, in which no glass ceiling presses down on the dreams of a child. Then we publish books for that world, where kids ask hard questions and we struggle with them together, where dreams stretch from eons ago into the future and we do our best to provide road maps to where these young folks want to be. We make books where the children of today can see themselves and each other. When presented with fences, with borders, with limits, with all the kinds of chains that hobble imaginations and hearts, we proudly say—no.

Text copyright © 2021 by Tina Cane
Jacket art copyright © 2021 by Yuta Onoda

All rights reserved. Published in the United States by Make Me a World, an imprint of Random House Children's Books, a division of Penguin Random House LLC, New York.

Make Me a World and the colophon are registered trademarks of Penguin Random House LLC.

Song permissions appear on page 324.

Visit us on the Web! GetUnderlined.com

Educators and librarians, for a variety of teaching tools, visit us at RHTeachersLibrarians.com

Library of Congress Cataloging-in-Publication Data is available upon request.
ISBN 978-0-593-12114-6 (trade) — ISBN 978-0-593-12116-0 (ebook)

The text of this book is set in 10.8-point Sabon MT Pro.
Interior design by Cathy Bobak

Printed in the United States of America
September 2021
10 9 8 7 6 5 4 3 2 1
First Edition

This book is dedicated to my children,
Cormac, Alma, and Titian.

Dear Reader,

Within the next two days, someone will ask you who you are.

It may happen in a government office or on an application. Perhaps you will take a test and write your name and student ID on top.

You may fill out a form online or maybe your computer will do it for you.

There may be something very important at stake. You may be in a doctor's office or at some boundary, border, or doorway, trying to find a safe place to sleep.

Or it could be so innocuous that you feel lucky to be asked such a question as, "What flavor of ice cream do you want?"

There is something beautiful about the alarming frequency of the questions. We live in a time when there is so much possibility—or rather, the possibilities within each of us are just a little closer to being recognized than they were in generations before yours.

While your ancestors may have been limited by their geography, or laws and customs concerning who they could choose to be, or money—or some combination of those factors—it is possible that you can, at the very least, imagine outside of the boundaries they were given.

But even within that expanding base of freedom, there is still an expectation that you will have answers to the question—and that the answers will be clear, definitive, and boundaried.

That you will not answer the question of who you are with another question, or a set of multiple identities, or something that changes from minute to minute.

Of course, this is, in fact, how identity works. One day you are eight years old, then, magically, you are nine. I am confident and decisive when I am drawing and painting, less so when I am ice-skating. (I am *never* confident when I am ice-skating.)

Alma is a young person who is growing up at the intersection of everything. The East Village in New York City in the '80s was a beautiful mash-up of possibility, danger, and selfhood. St. Marks Place was washed in graffiti, punk rock, hip-hop, and street vendors. Her own heart is drawn to every kind of narrative, from classical mythology to kung fu movies to David Bowie and Stevie Wonder. If you ask Alma who she is, you would be unlikely to receive the same answer twice.

This book asks the question, "What if who you are isn't a question you answer once and perfectly?" The answer doesn't always have a period at the end of the sentence. Sometimes, it ends in a question mark, or a slash. Sometimes, there are multiple conflicting answers.

Maybe that is the last bit of freedom that we are looking for, to know that we can change, that we can grow. That we are like music, or those street corners in New York City in the 1980s, where you never quite knew what would happen, and it was full of possibility, and it would be remarkable, and real, and full of life.

Like Alma, like you.

Christopher Myers

MAKE ME A WORLD

Thirteen

I was a thirteen-month-old baby once   now I'm a thirteen-

year-old girl   sometimes unlucky   like when a mirror

cracked   into shards in my backpack   and I saw my face

reflected back at me   in as many parts as I felt   I was

made of   as many as the number of times   my mother

told me a raw-edged hand mirror   like that was bound

to crack inside my bag   with my lunch box   banging up

against it   but did I listen?
                  no   I preferred

to steal glances at my hair   in the hall

between classes to make sure
                    my part was straight

                    my ponytail supersmooth

Lucky Unlucky

A broken mirror means bad luck   and there I was

carrying one around on my back all day   like a beast

of burden so that   my steps chimed like pocket change

but I was also lucky   not to slice the skin of my fingers

each time I reached in   to get a pencil or a brush

also lucky enough to move through the world   with a name

like Alma which means *soul*   meaning spirit   which I have

a lot of   or so I am told   which I prefer to believe

because it's a free country

                                    I can believe   anything I want

Talking Book

I know books can talk   because books talk to me   in my head

as I read in bed while my parents sleep late   in the other room

different from the *Talking Book*   I bought for four bucks

on St. Marks Place in downtown New York a few blocks

from where I live   it's a vinyl album   with Stevie Wonder

on the cover in perfectly parted cornrows

looking spiritual   as he ponders a patch of earth

ancient-seeming   old as dirt   *without sight but*

blessed with insight   which is what I once heard   a blind

man say   at Ray's Candy Store   as he made his way out

into the sunshine   on Second Avenue   a cane in one hand

a can of cream soda in the other

Places and People

It's strange how   places and people

can have power   how places and people

can change   how change can be scary

how places like people   have strengths

and have weaknesses   but how the center

can hold   if your center is a place

or people   you call *home*

Home

home
3a : a familiar or usual setting : congenial environment;
also : the focus of one's domestic attention
<*home* is where the heart is>
b : HABITAT
< The island is *home* to many species of birds.>

Your home and your people   involve choices and luck

they are also   what you make them

                                    home is not a house

but a place   not a structure   but a space

you can build   with your heart   and your mind

or any other way you find   not everyone is born *in* a home

or *to* a home

                but we are all born   unto ourselves

Superstition

superstition
1a : a belief or practice resulting from ignorance, fear of the
unknown, trust in magic or chance, or a false conception of
causation
b : an irrational abject attitude of mind toward the supernatural,
nature, or God resulting from superstition
2 : a notion maintained despite evidence to the contrary

My Chinese grandparents are superstitious in a way that feels

random to me   not random like   Stevie Wonder's

"Superstition"   Track 6 on *Talking Book*   where the song

is all about falling ladders   broken mirrors

and good luck   in the past

                  but random as in

Don't flip the fish   what my grandmother

snaps   in a sharp voice   before slapping me

on the wrist   with a pair of plastic chopsticks

When you're done eating one side   lift and discard

the spine with care   to avoid bad luck   a hundred

billion years of bad luck   I must have brought down

between that   and washing the oils from my scalp

on inauspicious days   and being half-white

and all girl   like a broken mirror   reflection

of a person that doesn't show you   what you want

or expect to see

Betting

Betting on horses   is a different kind   of *system of belief*

at the Belmont Stakes   Grandmother is all smiles and hand-

squeezing   passing me hard candies   from her purse

glossy ruby- or emerald-colored sweets   slightly melted

so the cellophane sticks to their sides   so I have to pry each

free with my teeth   as we ride the train to Elmont   at the races

Grandmother only puts her money on a horse   if she likes

its name
                Gazpacho   *Copernicus*   *Lady's Secret*

while Grandfather, all business   studies the *Daily Racing Form*

like a statistician   who always comes up short   even when our

horse is last   Grandmother presses two dollars into my palm

But look I say   *We lost!* pointing at the board   *Shhh* she hisses

as if the spirits will hear   as if it's more bad luck

Funny Not Funny

My Jewish grandma always told jokes   the Yiddish kind

which are funny   and not so funny   at the same time

like:

> There was a bar mitzvah where the rabbi stacked
> a bunch of apples on a table with a sign that said
> "Take only one apple, please. God is watching."
> On another table   there was a pile of cookies
> on which a friend of the bar mitzvah boy
> placed a sign saying   "Take all the cookies
> you want. God is watching the apples."

funny not funny   Grandma Miriam was always sweet with

her blue-gray bouffant   fresh from the salon each week

Entenmann's coffee cake   always in the fridge

once Grandma Miriam ironed   and burned my favorite socks

once she knit me a blanket with squares   colorful like

stained glass   once I gave her lice   three trips

to the beauty parlor   and a good story to tell

before Grandma Miriam passed away   she gave me

A Woman of Independent Means   by Elizabeth Forsythe Hailey

I didn't understand the book   but I think I understood

what she was trying to tell me

Kings Plaza

It was July   not long before Grandma Miriam died   I was

nine   and driving around   with my cousin Jonathan

from the Brooklyn side of my family   my elbow propped

on the passenger window of his Sunbird

                                    we were cruising

Kings Plaza at dusk   "How Deep Is Your Love" was on

the radio   I remember J said   *The Bee Gees sound like girls*

in a way that meant   he's the type of person   who might not

think girls run as fast   as they really do

                                    J was seventeen

wore cream-colored bell-bottom jeans   like John Travolta

a blue-eyed quarterback   from Sheepshead Bay   it seemed

to me he should have known more about girls   than he did

but I loved him   for playing Frisbee with me   on the field

across from Grandma Miriam's   for driving me down

Flatbush Avenue   as he stopped here and there   to chat up girls

with feathered hair   Jordache jeans and wide combs

in their back pockets   like the kind I wanted to get   that said

HOT STUFF and CURVES AHEAD

I remember it was humid   my hair felt thick   as a real

pony's tail   everything was electric   everyone friendly

and we were all smiling   feeling fine in a way   that even

when you're nine   you savor for the sense   that time

won't keep the moment   unless you do

Fifth Grade

In that class photo from fifth grade   in my flowered cotton dress

and stiff brown shoes   I have a big smile on my face   I don't

know why   it was not a happy time   but when I saw Sacagawea

in the social studies filmstrip   grainy and flickering on the screen

I was heartened to see   she had dark eyes like me   long hair

like mine   useful and intrepid   she was the kind of girl

I wanted to be   except for the part   about being kidnapped

and sold   then given as a child bride   to settle a bet

which is why I guess   Sacagawea was always pictured

pointing forward   because why would

she want to look back?

Ray's Candy Store

I slap two quarters   on the counter at Ray's   and point

at the Mary Janes   piled up in the plexiglass box   on the wall

of plexiglass boxes of sweets   Ray grabs a bag of Rolets

fried pork rinds   clipped to the shelf   because he knows

I can't reach them myself   I don't have enough change today

for a pineapple soda   next time I'll come with Clarissa

who's had "mug money"   pinned inside her parka   ever since

I've known her   she's never been robbed   so it's a waste

of a dollar   if you ask me   Ray stuffs my snack into a tiny

brown bag   says *See you later, Alma!*   as I hop on my bike

and hightail it   back to my block

Ray's Pizza

The Original   *The One and Only*   except for the thousand

other pizza places called *Ray's*   scattered across New York

a parlor it is not   but the high tables   make us feel

grown up   as we sit hunched   over steaming slices

which we hold folded at an angle   to drain off the grease

our paper plates supple   with that orange liquid

deliciousness   every day in evidence   on Principal Miller's

necktie as he smiles   from across his messy desk or from

behind the mic   in the auditorium where the whole

school watches rainy-day cartoons   which is better than

the puberty film   either way it's a total mayhem

of screaming delight   like *Watch out for the anvil!*

and *Elmer Fudd's got a gun!*   plus three hundred of us

doing the Woody Woodpecker laugh   all at the same time

is enough to drive any grown-up   out of their mind

but Mr. Miller's cool   he just sits in the back   before sneaking

out early   for his daily Ray's   to beat the noon rush of kids

lunch money bunched up   in their fists $1.10 for a slice

and small Coke   fifteen cents extra for Sicilian

Moving

We're moving again   my mom my dad and me   we don't have

much to move but still   we have to move it   down the block

to a larger apartment   where I can have a small room

of my own   and like most everything else   this involves

bickering

                            Why do you insist on keeping this?

                            That's not even mine!

even simple tasks   sometimes end with my mom   crying

in frustration   or my dad leaving for a long walk   to clear

his head   to try and understand why   what he said was

wrong   why there's always static   in the song of their life

together   like they can't hear the lyrics   or don't know

what they mean   like they speak different languages   or don't

know how to sing

                          I fold my clothes

fast pack my books   and my art supplies

into a cardboard box   then sit on the stoop   with my

Walkman on   so I can listen to something light

like disco or the Go-Go's   until my mom makes me

come back in   to wrap and stack the plates   each in a leaf

of *The Village Voice*   or *The New York Times*   until my fingers

are smudged   gray with newsprint   until my ears

are numb   to the sound   of their squabbling   and I can't

remember   what these rooms even looked like

with our stuff still in them

Mystery Achievement

Mystery achievement
Don't breathe down my neck, no

—The Pretenders, "Mystery Achievement"

There's heavy bass   in this Pretenders song   and I love it

I love it so much   I listen to it twelve times in a row   tapping

my foot   playing the drums in the air   in my new room

surrounded by boxes   and piles of clothes

                                                            this is my house

but sometimes I feel   more at home outside   *no breathing*

down my neck   no   riding around on my bike   or sitting

on a stoop   eating Red Hots   with Clarissa or Maureen

or Marta or Faith   we hang around and wait   as if something

is going to happen   but nothing really ever does   except

sometimes   I have a mysterious feeling   for no reason   intense

and emotional   as an emergency   like there's a lot going on

inside   that no one can see   that's when I stroll over

to a parked car   pretend to smooth my ponytail

in the reflection   of the rolled-up window   and try

to see   what's happening with me

Mystery: Miguel

You're on my mind
Every day, every nighttime I feel, yeah
Mystery achievement, you're so unreal

—The Pretenders, "Mystery Achievement"

Boys are a mystery   the way they act   the way they talk

sometimes kind and chill   sometimes rough and moody

I guess the same could be said of me   which is what Miguel

from my block says   when I don't feel like riding our bikes

to the store or to the yard   to watch the high school boys

play basketball   I don't always know why   I don't want to

I like Miguel   maybe even *like him* like him   I do know

it turns his mellow attitude   sort of stormy and mean   *Fine!*

he'll snap and snatch his bike up   from off the sidewalk

before booking down the street   *Wait!*   I'll shout

in my head   but never out loud   *Don't go! I just want*

to be alone
                which I realize

is what you'd call   a contradiction

Mystery: Grown-ups

Mystery achievement
Where's my sandy beach? Yeah
I had my dreams like everybody else
But they're out of reach
I said right out of reach
I could ignore you
Your demands are unending
I got no tears on my ice cream but you know me
I love pretending

—The Pretenders, "Mystery Achievement"

Grown-ups are a mystery   the way they act   the way they talk

sometimes kind and chill   sometimes rough and moody

I guess the same could be said of me   which is what my mom

and my dad say   when I read books   and don't feel like

talking   then want hugs   then refuse to do my chores

mercurial   is the word they use   which means always

changing   like the mercury in a thermometer   but I like

to think of Mercury   the messenger from mythology

with winged shoes and helmet   he ran faster than anyone

bearing messages   that rulers listened to   unlike

Cassandra   who had the gift of prophecy   but was ignored

by people like grown-ups   so busy   telling you what to do

and being right   that they can't even hear

what you're saying half the time

Lunar New Year

We celebrate 1982   the Year of the Dog   with Grandmother

and Grandfather   down on Hester Street   my mom doesn't

scrub the house   or cut my hair   the way most Chinese

mothers do   we just share a big meal   and I wear red

get red envelopes of cash   *hongbao* from my grandparents

which I plan to buy records and candy with

                                                    I feel like

we celebrate the holiday halfway   maybe because I am half-

Chinese   and my grandparents were not pleased   when my

mom married   outside of her tradition   they call my

dad *lofan*   which means *white devil*   he laughs

and says he doesn't mind   but I think   it pains him

inside   to be kept outside of something   so important

I halfway know   how he feels   the way every

Chinese family   wishes for a boy   makes me angry

the way left-handed (bad luck)   I tend to cross

my chopsticks (bad form) when I eat   but I think it's bad form

to call people devils   to wish that all your children are boys

Knishes

When it's cold out we like to bike   down East Houston

as a crew   to get potato knishes   for sixty-five cents

at Yonah Schimmel's
                                    wrapped in thin foil   each bundle

is instant comfort   in your pocket   reminding me of a book

I once read   about a girl who is poor   and walks to school

with baked potatoes   in her coat to keep warm   she eats

the potatoes for lunch at noon   while the other kids laugh at her

as if her mother's solution   isn't some kind of genius

as if there aren't worse things   you could call a person than

"Hot Potato Katie"   like "Skateboard"   which is what Miguel

called me the other day   when I told him to go away   he was

implying that my boobs   haven't come in   like Faith's

or Maureen's
                        Fine I said

but I'm the skateboard you'll never ride   *Oooh!* everyone cried

Dissed right in front of your own house!   *Word* I said

and biked toward home   smiling to myself   because even

I had to admit   that was a good one

Candy I Love

Now and Later

Lemonheads

Red Hots

Mary Janes

Kit Kat

Toffifay

Reggie Bar

York Peppermint Pattie

Green Apple Jolly Rancher

Tootsie Roll

Pop Rocks

Twizzlers

Blow Pop

Fire Ball

Starburst

Almond Joy

Twix

M&M's

Charleston Chew

Whatchamacallit

$100,000 Bar

Slo Poke

Rolo

Raisinets

Goobers

Butterfinger

Whoppers

Spree

Things I Want to Know

Are aliens real?

Will there be a nuclear war someday?

Does Miguel like me that way?

Why don't rich people give their money away?

Why is Clarissa's mom so sad?

And her dad so mad?

Does Cousin J really like Cheryl?

Or does he just think she's pretty?

Does Miguel like me?

Even if I can run faster than he can?

Even if I am sometimes smarter?

Banana Now and Later—why?

Daily Commute

Everyone on my block   goes to school near here   but I have

to cut across several avenues   to get to mine   ever since

we moved west to east   which is fine with me   because

those West Village kids   are still my people too

like Jennifer S.   who has flowered contact paper   in her

kitchen drawers   so that when you   reach for a spoon

roses bloom from between   all the silver handles

it's a detail I find beautiful   like the ivy vines growing

on the outside of her brownstone

                    how the buildings change

as I approach Fifth Avenue each day   everything turns

neat as a pin   as Grandma Miriam used to say   about her

hair   or anything that showed care   I can see there's a lot

of care taken on these streets   not like my block   where

the houses look shabby   and the people seem troubled

by life

          one day I came home from school

shaking my head   *What's going on?* my mother said

There's a couple of junkies   sleeping in the lot   I sighed

They're not junkies, honey   she said   *They're homeless*

Same thing, right? I said   *No* my mother shook her head

with a sad look on her face   *No no no*   like my mistake

contained a little bit of heartbreak

                                    which I guess it did

Maureen

Abject is the word   my mother uses to describe   how poor

Maureen's family is   *Like I "object" to being poor?*   I ask

Ab-ject she says   *It means extreme*   *as in extreme poverty*

Oh I say   *but I bet they still object* I add   *Yeah* she laughs

but she's not laughing   when I tell her about Maureen's

apartment   how it's completely bare   no furniture

anywhere   except for a card table   in the kitchen

and a wooden chair   where her grandpa sits   smoking

Kent cigarettes and drinking Schlitz beer   how there's a sticky

yellow plume on the wall   where his tin-lid ashtray   sends

up feathery signals   I imagine mean things like

Paint these dirty, cracking walls   Cover those light bulbs

Hang a curtain, please   but if there is any meaning to be

found   no one cares   it's a silent house   we're just there

to get Maureen's windbreaker   at first she tries to make us

wait in the hall   but we've been hanging out   for two years

and have never even seen her room
                              Come on

Clarissa elbows in with me   Marta and Faith

right behind her
all of a sudden

we stop short as if on a ledge   stand silent for a second

taking in all the emptiness   *Okay, Maureen   Just get*

your coat I say   *We gotta go*   but I had that picture

in my head   for the rest of the day   all that *abject-ness*

in one small space
just two floors up

from Clarissa's place   where there's a leather sectional

a TV and even Atari   it's true no one on our block has money

except for Faith   who goes to private school   Marta likes

to joke with her
Why you even here?

Faith just holds up   her middle finger and smiles   *Because*

I love you guys   it's true we don't care about who has what

or that Faith's parents get a case of gin   delivered to their

apartment every Friday   take vacations in a place called

Nantucket   which Clarissa calls *Nah-fuck-it*   but *abject*

scares me   I feel scared for Maureen   all she has at home

is dust   and even with her grandma's love   it doesn't seem

like enough

Hallway

Stuff always happens in hallways   a vestibule can be a cozy

placc   halfway between home and the street   the familiar

aroma of neighbors' cooking   *chuletas* or franks and beans

thick in the air
                        a dim light buzzing its last spark

circling inside the fluorescent light   humming above

our heads   on the landing where I have my first kiss

where the plaster wall   is warm against my back

and the tile cool beneath my feet   when I take off my flip-flops

as we sneak   around the stairs   away from Clarissa's door

taking a break from watching a movie   by sort of pretending

to play hide-and-seek
                        the hallway is where

Miguel tastes a little like peaches   when he kisses me

until he stops   for a second to say
                        Hey,

did you hear about   that waitress from the fourth floor

who got raped in the hall?   Jeez! Miguel!   I huff pushing

his hands   off my shoulders   I fast slide on my sandals

rush down the steps to get my bike

Alma! I hear him calling

What did I say?

Miguel sure knows how to ruin a moment   because of course

I knew   who didn't?   especially us girls

Andy Warhol

Andy Warhol is sitting across from me on the M14   looking

pale and fragile   sitting very upright   in his black turtle-

neck sweater and black sunglasses   even though it's not

sunny
                but he's a well-known artist

so maybe he doesn't want   to be recognized   he's also

wearing a faint smile   like he's pleased about something

private in his mind   kind of like the *Mona Lisa*   which is

the way I feel too   sitting across from Andy Warhol

with a plain view   of his bad skin   under what looks like

beige makeup   I feel strange about keeping   a giddy secret

near a famous stranger
                                        no one else on the bus

seems to know   that he is Andy Warhol   which is surprising

because everyone is old and Polish   just like him   I'm

wondering when and where   Andy got his first kiss

if he is thinking about this   like me   as we travel west

on Fourteenth Street   toward Union Square

Clarissa

It's hard to believe Clarissa is full-Chinese   the way she drinks

pickle juice   straight out of the jar from Guss's   we keep

saying her mom should just go   down to Orchard Street

buy her a barrel   and put it in the kitchen with a ladle

Clarissa doesn't even eat the pickles   only her sister does

so it works out   but

                              That's a lot of salt my mother says

And with all that soda she drinks   my mom adds   shaking

her head so I know   she's saying something more

than what she just said   I roll my eyes   thinking what

happened the other day   must be on her mind   how

Clarissa and I were at the laundry   where Clarissa's mother

works   hanging out   eating take-out white rice drizzled

with packets of soy sauce   another thing

my mother cannot abide

                              when Alisha

Clarissa's sister walks in   wearing her new Sergio Valentes

with the flashy gold horseshoes   embroidered on the butt

she also has lip gloss on   and her glasses off   so they don't

interfere   with the light blue eye shadow   smeared

on her lids   she looks loud but beautiful   Clarissa

and I sit staring   until their mother catches sight of this

rushes up and slaps Alisha to the floor   where Alisha remains

for a scary second too long   beside the stacked bags

of folded clothes   their safety-pinned tickets   flapping

in the wind of the fan
                              when Alisha finally gets up

she's holding her face   her mom is screaming something

in Chinese   as Alisha rushes out onto the street   *What'd she say?*

I ask Clarissa   leaning in, she whispers

> *It's dangerous to dress like that on our block*

On Our Block

Miguel is eating a Sugar Daddy   shining the golden Jesus head

he wears around his neck   with the end of his sleeve   I call it

his "Jesus in Pain"   he calls me names   claims I am

disrespecting God   *Your god, maybe* I say

Sad he says

shaking his head   whatever

On Our Block

Marta is speaking Spanish to Miguel   complaining about

her family in a way she thinks   only he can understand

Marta's mother says   Cubans and Puerto Ricans   aren't

supposed to get along   but Miguel and Marta   must share

something deep   through the way they speak   because

whenever stuff is going on   Marta talks to Miguel

nobody else

On Our Block

Faith in her plaid skirt and white shirt   with the dainty round

collar split like two half-moons   is jamming the elevator button

with her thumb   in a rush to get upstairs   so she can change

into jeans and Keds   she never wants to miss anything

always feels like she's missing out   with her school being

so far uptown   but it seems like we're the ones   with the short

end of the stick

                             as much as she is one of us

Faith's life is mysterious in ways   we don't really even get

like how a diplomat's son   stole some equipment   from

the computer lab at her school   *Computer lab?*   we asked

                                  What's that?

On Our Block

Marta is beautiful   with her little gold hoops   and long

glossy braid   how she can be telling a story   about butterflies

in her grandfather's garden in Bayamón   slip into Spanish

for a second   to say one juicy word   that we don't know

but totally understand   because of the way   she is using

her hands   we can see she means   *fragile* and *magical*

which is also sometimes Marta

On Our Block

Maureen = 100 percent Irish + quiet and loyal and smart

Irish as the day is long   Faith's mother once said   plus

something else   about *shanty* and *lace curtains*   which

we didn't get
                              Erin go bragh!

is what Dario from around the corner   sometimes hollers

when he snaps   Maureen's bra strap   through her T-shirt

as he cruises by on his bike   *Get off our block!*   we shout

at his back   as he turns right   onto Second Avenue

He likes you   we tell Maureen   but she doesn't seem to care

she likes Chinese jump rope   and braiding my hair   while

sitting on the steps of my building

                                        she also maybe likes Miguel

On Our Block

There are many names   for the women who stand in doorways

while their boyfriends pace the street   none of those names

are anything you'd want to say   so everybody's parents

just call them "the Girls"   like when they call the police

they ask
                    Would you please have a car come around?

The Girls are back   Sure the cops always say

but a couple of hours later   the Girls return anyway

some of them are even friends   with the police   are sometimes

seen getting out of their patrol cars   in the middle of the day

What's up with that?   the kids want to know   but the parents

just roll their eyes   reach for the phone   in a way that tells us

the answer is more complicated   than they are willing

to explain
                    Just worry about yourself

my mother tells me   and I do   because some of those women

are actually girls   not much older than me   and look a little feral

beneath their heavy makeup   blue like a bruise   in the late-afternoon   shadowy doorways   they look kind of wounded

like Alisha's eyes looked   when she ran out of the Laundromat

holding her cheek   the day her mother hit her   for dressing

like that   the word itself a slap   which is why we say *Girls*

which is what they are   what we are too

Litterbug

We're taking the train to Thirty-fourth Street   to see this movie

Diner   which me and Clarissa   and Faith and Maureen

have already seen three times   Miguel is with us   why?

no one knows   because we're not a thing   and since when

does he see movies uptown?

                                   but whatever   he's there

on the platform   kicking the pillar   and now he's tossing

his Twix wrapper onto the tracks   *Hello?* I say pointing

You shouldn't litter   You sound like that poster he laughs

"Don't Be a Litterbug!"   Well, yeah I sigh   *It's illegal*

It's illegal Miguel mimics me   *You're like that Indian on the TV*

commercial   crying about throwing trash in the woods

he snorts

                          Native American I say   *It's crying Native American*

Native whatever he grumbles   *Wow* I huff   and move

to step into the car   *Wow*

On Our Block

There's our apartment   where my mom is frying pork

in her wok   smoking a Marlboro cigarette   where her hair

long and black   lies flat on her back   in a way that mine

does not   mine being lighter   and somewhat wavy

especially when it rains

There's also my mom   filling out my permission slip   in her

graceful Catholic school cursive   so that I can go

on the eighth-grade trip   to Ellis Island   and there she is

signing my report card   smiling lightly   to let me know

she's proud

Here is my mother   smoothing my ponytail   with slender

fingers   saying as she often does   *You know you can*

do anything   then waiting   for me to respond   *I know*

I know   the way she taught me to long ago   there's also

Mom handing me the phone   eight o'clock at night

whispering *It's a boy*   trying not to laugh   when my

eyes go wide   before she lights a cigarette

and wanders into the kitchen   so that I can have

                                    some privacy

Mom brushing her hair before bed   looking pretty but

careworn   in her flowered robe   out of her office blouse

work skirt and pantyhose   lonely-seeming sometimes

with my dad working nights   her book of stories

by Flannery O'Connor   heavy on the nightstand   stories

like "A Good Man Is Hard to Find"   "The Life You Save

                                    May Be Your Own"

My mother handing me   a box of Blue Tip matches   saying

Go ahead   You light the oven   precisely because she knows

I am afraid of the way   the gas silently builds up   as I hesitate

I can feel her waiting   for the sound of the strike

of the match   for the orange flash   fast like a time-lapse

flower   sped up but muted   a *whoosh* reaching

to singe my lashes   hushed as my mother

blowing smoke   through her nose

On Our Block

My dad heads out around two o'clock   walks west toward

Tenth Avenue   to the taxi garage   where he rents

his medallion   for a twelve-hour shift   four nights

a week   which means I mostly see him on weekends

which is fine   because our place is small   and when we're

all at home it feels crowded   and sometimes heated too

by a low simmer of disappointment   that my dad's still

driving a cab   even though   he'd rather do anything

but drive

           back when Grandma Miriam was alive

it made her crazy   the way my dad wouldn't just quit   the way

his classmates grew up   to become doctors and lawyers

my mom used to joke   it was like that off-off-Broadway play

My Son the Waiter: A Jewish Tragedy   but she doesn't joke

anymore   or laugh when my dad calls himself *downwardly*

mobile   says he really only wanted   to travel and see the world

which he did for many years   which my mother calls

just another form of dreaming   all I know is

whether he wants to or not   my dad keeps driving

like his life   depends on it

Latchkey

Everyone on my block is a *latchkey kid*   which is a term I just

learned from Ms. Nola   the guidance counselor at my school

I overheard her   talking in the office   to Vice Principal Gordon

Well, there's a fair number of latchkey kids   she said

There's no one in the house when they get home

                                  all of a sudden

Mr. Gordon started talking about numbers   which made me

wonder if he even heard what she said   made me think

of that expression   *a house is not a home*   which I get

because a home should be full of music   cooking

smells and kitchen sounds and footsteps overhead

when I think *latchkey*

                  I see a lone spoon on a table

                a single napkin   a half glass of water

some of the younger kids   still wear their keys on string

around their necks   have their bus passes pinned

to their jackets for safekeeping   I'm smiling to myself

imagining kids walking around   wearing spoons

when Mr. Gordon points at me   *Why are you here?*

he wants to know   *Mimeograph machine*

I say   waving a sheet of paper

Walkman

My mom and dad gave me a Walkman   when I turned thirteen

it was the best thing   that ever happened to me   I am not sure

they would agree   annoyed as they often are   that I go around

with my headphones on   most of the time   when I am at home

even when I am reading   my dad loves to read   and can't

understand my doing   two things at once   or that my Walkman

contains the mixtape of my life   that I like the company

of other people's voices   alongside what I am doing or thinking

how when I am reading   I hear myself read-speaking the words

the characters think-speaking their feelings   and with a track

like Blondie's "Heart of Glass"

> Once I had a love and it was a gas
> Soon turned out had a heart of glass

overlaying the scene   the whole thing turns into   a chorus

of emotion   so that my heart and my brain feel full   and I have

to smooth my ponytail
                          just to get a grip

Mixtape

I buy mixtapes on St. Marks Place   with the Chinese New Year

money my grandmother thinks   I am saving for college   but

it's only ten dollars   and college is far away

                                        I can't wait to get

a bootleg recording of *The Clash Live in Cardiff 1977*

It's called "present-day orientation"   Alisha explains

meaning I am impatient   which I am   but at two for five

dollars   I don't think it's wrong   to want an extended

version   of "Police and Thieves" in my ear   as I rewind

cassettes with a pencil on the bus   or read about how

Anne Frank got her first kiss   on April 15, 1944

the exact day a year later   that the Bergen-Belsen camp

where she met her death   was liberated by British soldiers

Books

Now that I am done with *The Diary of Anne Frank*   which

made me cry   as I was writing my report   for Ms. Foster

who scribbled *Passionate!*   in purple pen in the margin

I've been reading *Deenie* by Judy Blume   *Are You There, God?*

It's Me, Margaret and *Blubber*   I have the whole set

in alphabetical order   on the shelf near my bed   I like

Judy Blume   because she gets how a girl might feel

about being teased for being fat   or having a crooked back

or for being confused about if   god exists or which to believe in

I guess if I had to choose a god   it would be books   because they

tell you everything   you'd ever want or need to know   without

any rules about   what you should be doing   who you should

like   or how you should think

even though fiction is made up

it contains a certain kind of truth   the kind that doesn't always

need *supporting evidence*   which is what I have to give

when I write an essay for Ms. Foster   which ruins reading

if you ask me   because I am not a lawyer   I am a reader

and it's plain to see   why Anne Frank liked Peter

and why he liked her   the evidence being that

                         I am a girl and I read the book

Agnostic

agnostic
1 : a person who holds the view that any ultimate reality
(such as God) is unknown and probably unknowable;
broadly : one who is not committed to believing in either the
existence or the nonexistence of God or a god
2 : a person who is unwilling to commit to an opinion about
something <political *agnostics*>

Why I ask my dad   *don't rich people give some of their money*

away   to even things out?   he smiles *That's called socialism*

Not everybody believes in it   but your grandpa Eli did

So he gave all his money away? I say   my dad laughs

He didn't have any money to give   Maybe that's why he was

a socialist I add   *I think you're onto something* says my dad

Was he agnostic like you?   I want to know   *Well, maybe*

"atheist" is the word I would use   Eli was pretty convinced

we were it   What do you mean by "it"? I ask   *That people*

are all there is   my dad says

                              I don't know I sigh

scanning the skyline   my eyes stop at the top   of the Con Ed

Building on Fourteenth Street   *I think there's got to be*

something out there   my dad laughs and tugs my ponytail

Well, then you may be agnostic too   at least for today

Extraterrestrials

Faith and I are up on the roof   of her apartment building

snuggled up   in these tubes of green fabric   that her

mother bought   at a remnants store on Orchard Street

not far from where   my own mom once bought a stack of tags

with my name printed on them   so I wouldn't lose my clothes

at day camp   it took one whole evening   for my mom to sew

them on by hand   and it so happened   that I didn't lose

a thing
                tonight, though

Faith and I look like   caterpillars   in our fabric tubes

not like the alien enthusiasts we are   with our copy

of *Chariots of the Gods*   a flashlight and a family-size bag

of M&M's   for our mission under a blue-black sky

dotted with so many bright stars   it seems even here

in the East Village   there's promise of life elsewhere

of extraterrestrials   whose possibility makes Earth

feel a little more like Earth   than it usually does   which

is difficult to explain

tonight we see a lot of planes

but no spaceships   even though we spend a lot of time

praying with our hands clasped   chanting *Please, give us a sign*

which I guess is *supporting evidence*   that I am agnostic

not atheist   I may be socialist too

Radio

I switch off   between 95.5 WPLJ and 98.7 KISS-FM   because

I prefer to mix things up   different music for different moods

at school   people tend to hang out in groups   according

to the type of music they like   like Josh in Mr. Richter's class

who's carving DISCO SUCKS! into his desk   with the sharp end

of his compass   claims to hate hip-hop   always sticks

with the punk rock kids   but I know Josh likes Grandmaster

Flash and the Furious Five   because he and I were singing

"The Message" on the stairs last week

> Don't push me 'cause I'm close to the edge
> I'm tryin' not to lose my head

with each line our eyes were getting wider   because we couldn't

believe how much of the song we knew   we were laughing really

hard by the time we were through   like we were instant friends

over this song   in spite of Josh's   love for the Sex Pistols

who I like too   for when I am angry or riding my bike

after my parents have a fight   or just feeling restless

of two minds on certain things

                              such as music and life

Signs

Clarissa is a Scorpio   Marta's a Libra   Maureen and Faith

are Aries   I'm a Gemini   and we all shout *Totally!*

when we realize   it's the sign of the Twins   because

although I'm an only child   Grandma Miriam once said

You're of two minds   and you'll need both of them   for all

the thinking you do

my friends on the block agree

there's definitely   a couple of kinds of me   the same way

we recognize Clarissa's temper   as a Scorpio's sting   handed

down from her mom   how we trace Marta's fear of fights

to the death of her cousin   who was killed at a club in San Juan

and Faith's hatred of confrontation to her parents   who pretend

even obvious things   are not happening

it's also

how we know   Maureen's tendency to share   is a gift

from her grandmother   who has nothing to give

but is generous   nonetheless

Kinds of Twins

There's Gemini Twins   Twin Donut   the Twin Towers

looming like tombstones   as my dad always says   and there's

twins like Yvonne and Yvette   who dress entirely alike

head to toe   all in one color every day   *monochromatic*

is the term   my art teacher Ms. Pierce would use   if she lived

around the corner from me   like Yvonne and Yvette do

whose mom shops   at the 69¢ Store on Eighth Street

for their accessories   because how else would she find

or afford matching yellow plastic   hoops and headbands

flip-flops or tube socks and skippies   or bangles and barrettes

all red or all blue   right down to the shoes   so cool

with their own private language   on their block

or at school   Yvonne and Yvette   speak to almost

no one
          but nod *Hey* to me

at Ray's sometimes   because as Faith says   they think

I am part Puerto Rican   on account of my olive skin

Sybil

Tara and I   live at opposite ends of the Village

me East   she West   so when we want to spend time together

we sometimes take the train   to Midtown after school

to visit the Museum of Broadcasting   just a few blocks

up from the library   with the giant stone lions

where we watch   all huddled up in a cubicle   with big

headphones on   any television show we want   from

the endless shelves of tapes   lining its bright corridors

we bring candy   which we crunch quietly   because

NO FOOD OR DRINK ALLOWED   but no one is ever there anyway

except for the lady at the desk   who practically rolls her eyes

when the elevator opens   and she sees us coming

leaning into each other   already laughing   it's probably

because we're so loud   as we watch old *Love Boat* episodes

or tragic *Afterschool Special*s   where a teen is always suffering

from an incurable disease or unrequited love   silly shows we eat

up like Twizzlers   fast without thinking   because there's

not much there   but still delicious   plastic with a hint

of sweet
        lately we're into

In Search of . . . conspiracies and mysteries like King Tut's tomb

or the lost Mayans or the threat of killer bees   today

though   we're watching a movie called *Sybil*   starring

Sally Field   and it's freaking us out   because her mom

is mean and scary   and how can one person possess

multiple personalities?   but it's based on the true story

of Sybil's mind turning her into other people   in order

to deal when she's stressed
                        Wow we keep whispering

clutching each other in the cubicle   *This is messed up*

Chinatown

I hate how the fish market   smells like fish   how difficult

it is for me   to feel relaxed   walking with my grandmother

through the crowd   as she inspects the sea bass   dead-eyed

and draped over mounds of crushed ice   pink in places

from where the blood and guts seep down

                                            I hate how

the new fishmonger watches me   sideways with a curiosity

I sense sometimes in Chinatown   as he strips a fish of its scales

he must see how my hair   is not quite black   but chocolate

brown   my eyes not the *rice eyes*   a kid on the bus

once scowled at me   but wide enough to be   from halfway

across the world

                        Lofan?

I know the man is wondering   but not asking outright   like

some shopkeepers might   how neighbors have in the past

I'm okay with that now   even if my grandmother still bristles

a little   pressing cash against the fishmonger's palm   faster

than she has to   shoving the bass wrapped in newspaper

into her string bag   before grabbing my hand to leave

Starburst

One night when I was nine   after a dinner at the dumpling

house in Chatham Square   I walked the whole length

of Mulberry Street   holding each of my parents' hands

while squinting my eyes   not shut supertight   but gently

squeezed   to look more naturally Chinese   it was

dizzying to me   how the light from the streetlamps

and neon storefronts   splintered like firecrackers

frozen in midair   or stars stuck bursting   in the night

sky   I feel silly now   remembering that time

like:

       Starburst is a candy I love

       not how I want to see the world

How I Met My Grandmother

I was eight and coloring   a scene from *Star Wars*   with my big

box of Crayola crayons   the kind with the lousy plastic

sharpener that shaves each crayon   blunt as a stick

when my grandmother walked in

                                just like that

there she was   a not-so-old Chinese lady   standing

before me   shopping bags at her feet   a black pleather purse

on her wrist   she came over   held my face for a second

gave me a kiss   then went into the kitchen   put on

my mother's apron   and fired up the wok

                                Who's that?

I asked *That's your grandmother*   my mom said

as she lit a cigarette   and left to unload the groceries

it was my dad's day off   so when I heard the gate slam

I rushed out into the hall   to catch him   before he got

to our door

                 Dad I whispered   *Mom's mom is here*

Wow, okay he said   smoothing his hair   and clearing

his throat   before turning the knob   from that

moment on   no one talked about it anymore

just acted like my grandmother   had always been with us

which in a way
                    I guess she had

Mythology

Is tricky   *Mythology* by Edith Hamilton especially

because Ms. Foster is very detail-oriented   gives daily quizzes

about Hades   and the curse of the House of Atreus

I have trouble   keeping all the names straight   the gods

and their relationships are complicated   like every family

I guess   minus the stuff   about cooking up your relatives

which is what Tantalus does   to his own son Pelops

whose shoulder gets munched   at the banquet

by Demeter   who at first doesn't notice   sad as she is

about her daughter Persephone   being kidnapped

and taken   to Hades the place   by Hades the god

See? confusing
                         These people are crazy Josh calls out

as the class laughs   Ms. Foster explains that they aren't people

but gods   that the way of the gods   is wrath and payback

that myths are meant   to teach us mortals lessons about life

like how my dad always says   *Success is the best revenge*

but since   he is the least vengeful person   I know

this advice doesn't sound very useful

Dreams

My dad may not know much about revenge   but he knows

a lot about dreams   and always tells me   what mine mean

when I tell him about the one I had   not long ago   where I am

a deer being chased   deep into the woods   he laughs and says

That's about boys   *Next?*   *How is that about boys?*   I object

It's about me being afraid of being chased   I protest

I rest my case he smiles   sliding his glasses down his nose

You don't know   I say waving my hand   *Any others?* he asks

There is this one I have pretty often   *about a house burning*

down to the ground   *with giant orange flames*   *shooting out*

of the windows   *I think it's about the fall of the House of Atreus*

I say   *Yeah* he sighs   *Maybe that one's about your house*

Our house, I mean he adds   *How things between your mom*

and me   *are not always very peaceful*

                                        I think silently

on this for a minute   my dad watches me from across

the table   sipping his coffee   as my eyes tear up a little

Okay I nod

                    when he reaches over   and squeezes

my hand   *Okay* I squeeze back   *I understand*

Quentin Crisp

It's difficult to describe Quentin Crisp   who I see sitting

on a bench   near St. Mark's Church sometimes   when

I am riding my bike   to Gem Spa for a cherry soda

or an egg cream
                                Quentin is sort of fascinating to me

an old writer   who wears eyeliner and silky scarves   like

an elderly lady from the Upper East Side   but he's confusing

to someone like my grandmother   she won't even let me look

at the dwarf   who paints tourist portraits   on the streets

of Chinatown
                        as if whatever

made him short is catching   as if it's more bad luck

but Quentin Crisp seems harmless   with his wispy lavender

hair floating around his head   like a misty halo beneath

his black fedora
                        It's the makeup says Clarissa

Too much eyeliner   but I think it looks fine   his hair

reminds me   of the faint blue bouffant   Grandma Miriam

used to wear   she wouldn't have cared   that Quentin is gay

Live and let live she'd always say   she wasn't prejudiced that way

like Dario   who calls out names   as he rides by on his bike

never saying the words   quite loud enough   for Quentin

to look up   but I imagine he hears   or feels them

the way Jackie Robinson still heard   and felt the cruel

words being hurled at him   when he was up to bat

at the plate   even though his wife used to   shift her weight

move her body   to block the sounds   of the shouts

from the stands
                              I think Dario may be

more of a coward   than even those men   because

if you are going to name-call   you should at least

stand tall and claim it

Grandpa

My grandpa Eli died when I was six   I don't remember much

about him   but that he used to shuffle   across the kitchen

in his brown leather slippers   toward Grandma Miriam

whose outstretched hands   always held a small plate

with a piece of chocolate babka   or an apricot

hamantaschen on it

                        his death from Alzheimer's

was long and slow   the day of his funeral   I wasn't allowed

to go   so I sat on the screened-in porch   at their house

in Flatbush, Brooklyn   with my feet raised up   in Eli's

black recliner   where I fell asleep   and had a dream

about ants crawling over me

Grandfather

Is what I call my mom's dad   we never really talk

but sometimes   he gives me cash   which my mom

says is his way of showing he cares   which he does

insists my dad   who calls him
                                        a tough nut to crack

my mom tells me   that Grandfather had a hard life

back in China   that he lived   on the streets

of Guangzhou   for a while as a child   after his mother

died   which is about as much   as anyone knows

except for maybe Grandmother   who married him young

when they were both sixteen   after meeting him only once

at a park with her parents   before their wedding

was arranged
                         which is strange

as if she were being given away   as if love is a contract

not a feeling   even so they make a good team   get along

just fine   unlike my parents   who chose to be together

and still can't agree on anything

Ms. Nola

Wears big hoop earrings   a natural Afro   and a pen behind

her ear   I am waiting for her   to be done speaking

with Mr. Gordon   who's in the hall   waving a bunch

of papers   outside the frosted glass   of her office door

which from my side reads: **Ms. Nola, Social Worker**

on the wall   behind Ms. Nola's swivel chair   there's

a poster that says

> *We Are All Just Walking Each Other Home*
> *—Ram Dass*

What kind of name is Ram Dass?   I am wondering   when

Ms. Nola walks in   brisk and elegant as always   in her black

blazer with the big shoulder pads   and her sparkly brown eyes

that give you a feeling   she understands anything   you want

to share   because *that*   she declares   is her mission

Ms. Nola is a good listener   when she does her weekly check-ins

with each kid   sitting behind her desk   with her arms

outstretched   her hands open   over her stacks of folders

she always begins   with a wide smile

and a *What's going on?*

What's Going On

What's going on is this:

     I have been reading

The Book of Lists published in 1977 and which has sat

ever since on the table next to the potted jade plant

near our television set

     it's a fat paperback

filled with random facts lists like:

 People Who Died While Having Sex

 People Who Became Words

 Cases of Spontaneous Combustion

I tell Ms. Nola that sometimes I make lists of things I like

or things I want to know that if Anne Frank had made a list

it would have included items like this:

     hair curlers

     handkerchiefs

     schoolbooks

     a comb

     old letters

That unlike the poster tacked up   on Ms. Nola's bulletin board

which proclaims   in rainbow letters:

I WILL

BE YOUNG

AND

I WILL

SURVIVE

Anne Frank did not survive   even though she tried

and maybe Ms. Nola   should take down that poster

because it's basically a lie   as I say this

                                        my voice

breaks a little   and I am surprised   to hear I sound

kind of angry   to the point   where I am almost shouting

which is shocking   so to change the subject   I start

talking about   my recurring dream of the burning

house

            that my dad says is *our house*

and then about a new dream   where my mother eats my

uncle's shoulder   how I think that's because   I read about

the curse of the House of Atreus   which I am worried

means my house too

because these stories

are about gods   but filled with symbols for humans

who are kind of dumb   to take wisdom from

when I am done

Ms. Nola exhales   as if she had been holding her breath

Right on, Alma she says   *You are alive in the world*

with all the feelings   and it's a beautiful thing to see

then she smiles   *How about you make some lists for me?*

and I'm like *Great, homework*

List for Ms. Nola: Things
I Like About Myself

I am a strong reader

I am a good writer

I am a good biker

I am a good friend

I am a fast runner

I can light our messed-up oven

List for Me: Books I Love

The Dictionary

The Thesaurus

The Diary of a Young Girl by Anne Frank

The Outsiders by S. E. Hinton

Everything Judy Blume has written

A Wrinkle In Time by Madeleine L'Engle

Matilda by Roald Dahl

All Creatures Great and Small by James Herriot

Stuart Little by E. B. White

Charlotte's Web by E. B. White

The Trumpet of the Swan by E. B. White

The Secret Garden by Frances Hodgson Burnett

Anne of Green Gables by Lucy Maud Montgomery

The Pigman by Paul Zindel

The Effect of Gamma Rays on Man-in-the-Moon Marigolds by Paul Zindel

Pardon Me, You're Stepping on My Eyeball! by Paul Zindel

All the Little House books by Laura Ingalls Wilder

<u>Flowers in the Attic</u> by V. C. Andrews

<u>Chariots of the Gods?</u> by Erich von Däniken

<u>A Woman of Independent Means</u> by Elizabeth Forsythe Hailey

List for Ms. Nola: Things
I Wish I Could Change

For my hair
to be more straight   and more black and less unruly

For my school
to be closer   so I'd have a two minute walk
with friends from my block

For our apartment
to have many rooms filled with windows
to open for fresh air and many doors to close for privacy

For my father   to have a job he loves
For my parents   to get along

For my grandmother   to teach me mah-jongg
like Clarissa's grandma did

For Grandma Miriam   to return from the dead one day
just to say hello and that she loves me more than I'll ever know

Cooking

parable :
a usually short fictitious story that illustrates
a moral attitude or a religious principle

My mother likes   to speak in parables sometimes   meaning

she'll tell me   a random story about life   then leave it

to me   to figure out the point   which is irritating

especially if we are cooking   which is what we are doing

right now   soaking dried tiger lilies in a bowl   so they can be

simmered with chicken wings   in my mom's giant wok

and eaten over rice

                         we're recalling how

Grandma Miriam was an enthusiastic cook   who made terrible

food   how that made us   love her even more   *Remember*

when I gave her lice? I laugh

                         Yes my mom says

She was a good sport about that   *It's too bad she never taught*

your father to cook, though   Yeah I say   *But a lot of men*

don't cook   *True* my mother says   *But a lot of men do*

If you were my son   I would still be teaching you how

to make your own food   I don't want a child of mine

to end up   like the boy with no salt
                                    You mean

the boy who cried wolf? I ask   No my mom repeats

The boy with no salt
                    See, when your grandfather

was an orphan   living on the streets   he met an urchin

who was starving   So your grandfather showed him a market

stall where late at night   they could steal salt   without getting

caught   because as everyone knows   you'll never starve if you

have salt in the house
                    What? I snort

Everyone does not know that!   Well, they should says my mom

And now you know   so there's no excuse
                                    For what? I ask

Never mind she says   *So the boy filled his pocket and bid*

your grandfather goodbye   But there was a hole

in his pocket   and he left a trail of salt   behind him

wherever he went   which in the end   led to an alley

in Guangzhou   where the boy was found   dead

of dehydration   Because salt is also good

for water retention   So there you go   my mother concludes

There you go, what? I laugh   *That whole thing* I shake my head

doesn't even make sense   You mean I add *he died of dehydration*

in one night?
                    Just think about it my mom says

I am so *not thinking about that* I snort   *Well, then think*

about slicing ginger   she gestures with her cleaver

Those slices are way too thick

Mars

But her friend is nowhere to be seen
Now she walks through her sunken dream

    —David Bowie, "Life on Mars"

Every once in a while   Faith goes missing   not like

in the summer   when she ships off to Nantucket

for two whole months   but gone from our block

for a few days   now and then   when she's stuck in her

apartment   tending to her parents   after as my dad

says   *they've gone on a bender*   meaning they've had

too much to drink   for too long   and they have to stay

in bed   because of splitting headaches
                           on those days

Faith tiptoes around the house   fixing her mom and dad

eggs and coffee   until they feel like themselves again   ready

to open another shipment of gin   which means Friday

which means Saturday night   Faith and I are back up

on the roof   snuggled up in our tubes   listening to Bowie

on our Walkmen

Changes　　(*Turn and face the strange*)

Oh, you pretty things

(*You're driving your mamas and papas insane*)

or the song where he wonders　　if there's life on Mars　　which seems

foolish to ask　　because when you look at the sky　　then look back

to Earth　　the only answer　　is an obvious question

How can there not be?

Kung Fu Movies

One of Grandmother's favorite things in the world

aside from the Yankees   is a kung fu double feature

at the Sun Sing Theatre in Chinatown   so we go every

once in a while   on a Saturday afternoon   with a bag of tangy

preserved plums   big enough to last   the whole four hours

and since the movie house   is always really loud   we never

have to worry   about the sounds   we make tearing open

the waxy paper
                                    and since the place

is always trashed   we can throw our wrappers and pits

on the floor beneath our seats   without feeling bad   amid

the dozen conversations in Chinese   always happening

around us   as if there isn't even a film on   as if the star

isn't using her superlong braids   like a lasso to tie up

or knock out her foes
                                    Grandmother translates

and whispers to me   parts of the dialogue   I may need

to understand the story   even though   it's mostly action

which as Grandma Miriam used to say   *speaks louder than words*

Kung Fu Fighting

Dario is riding around in circles   looking like a doofus

on his supersmall bike   shouting the lyrics

to "Kung Fu Fighting" at me

> *Everybody was kung fu fighting*
> *Those cats were fast as lightning*

Clarissa is French-braiding my hair   on her stoop   I wave

my hand at Dario   like I don't care and I don't   but when

he starts squinting his eyes   and making *ching-chong* sounds

the way they chime in the song   I stand up   shake off

Clarissa's hand   that's still grasping the elastic   to shout

Don't you know that's racist?   Dario skids sideways to a stop

shrugs   says in disbelief
> *How can that be racist?*

It's in the song!
> *What the . . . ?* Clarissa and I say in unison

then break out laughing   because we can't believe

how stupid   and when I tell Clarissa   about the rest

with the *funky Chinamen*   and *funky Chinatown*

we shake our heads   saying *Damn*   as we watch Dario

weave his way back   around the corner

onto Second Avenue   and out of sight

Kung Fu

Kung fu is a state of mind   not just the martial arts part

but the practice of daily life   even simple tasks   like brushing

your teeth   my grandfather believes   can be kung fu

like if you're going   to brush your teeth   *brush them*

don't do things halfway   kung fu means   time and energy

and life requires   hard work and discipline
                                     only

my grandfather didn't tell me this   my mom does

when I ask her why   Grandfather won't acknowledge

his arthritis
               she says   *He thinks he can will it away*

which if you ask me   is the opposite of kung fu   but maybe

not so different   from how   when my mother says

You can do anything   I believe her   because why wouldn't I?

                         if given the choice

Ambivalent

Some things just come together   like when Ms. Foster includes

the word *ambivalent* on the list   for our vocabulary quiz

and it describes exactly   how I feel today

> AMBIVALENT
> *adjective*
> : having or showing simultaneous and contradictory
> attitudes or feelings toward something or someone :
> characterized by ambivalence

thinking about last week   when Miguel and I   were at his

house   sitting on the couch   trying to watch TV   I was

wondering   if he was going to kiss me again   even though

I wasn't completely sure   I wanted that to happen   I was pretty

clear on the fact   that I didn't feel like watching   *Knight Rider*

a show about a guy   with a talking race car   *How about*

Little House? I suggested   crouching down by the channel dial

Little House on the Prairie? Miguel laughed   *Too corny!*

But I loved that show   when I was little I said

And I've read every book   by Laura Ingalls Wilder

So? It still sucks   Miguel's laugh right then   felt like a stab   I don't really care if he   likes *Little House*

but I want him to care about me   even if we don't

agree on certain things   so I was thinking that maybe

Miguel isn't very kind   if he makes fun of something

I obviously like
                        when he leaned over to kiss me

we had half settled on *Family Feud*   but I wasn't

in the mood for stupid games
                        so I got up and left

Miguel acted offended   but I heard him   quick switch

to *Knight Rider*
                        as soon as I closed his apartment door

Serendipity

Is a fancy dessert café   on the Upper East Side

where I once went   with my parents on Easter Sunday

for chicken potpie   and frozen hot chocolate

it's also a word   that Grandma Miriam taught me:

> SERENDIPITY
> *noun*
> : the faculty or phenomenon of finding valuable
> or agreeable things not sought for

she was describing   how she met Grandpa Eli   which was

serendipitous because she had missed   her Manhattan-bound

A train to Times Square   where she was going   to interview

for a job in a typing pool   which in 1917   was a room filled

with women sitting at typewriters   wearing red lipstick

typing one hundred words per minute   with bells ringing

every two seconds   the rasp of paper being pulled   fast

from rollers   plus everyone having to holler   over the type-

writer clatter about war   in the trenches   and what their

sweethearts had mentioned   in their letters back home

War

Grandpa Eli never talked   about the First World War

which he fought in   or about Poland   the ghetto he left

at fourteen   or if he did   he never spoke about it

to me
        I was only six when he died

but I remember Grandma Miriam   on the afternoon

of his funeral   standing at the stove   stirring a pot

the sight of her back shaking   as she ladled chicken soup

into a bowl   and the tears in her eyes   but the smile

on her face   when she turned to me   as I sat waiting

at the table   listening to my parents   argue in her yard

Civil War

Marriage is a union   but I think maybe   it's actually a kind

of war   like the Civil War   which even had a Union side

which in my mind   was about letting people be free   not like

the Confederacy which decided   it was its own country

just so the South could keep its slaves

                                        Mr. Richter

who lives for social studies   says when we look across history

we see war   as an *ongoing state*   that at any given moment

there's a war going on somewhere in the world

                                                    like

the conflict in my kitchen   right now   there's always

a struggle for power   over who gets to do what

and when   over who decides   what we have for dinner

or when we have it   who has to make more money

shop for groceries   over who should stop complaining

about driving a cab   and just get another job   who should stop

worrying about making her parents mad   and just live

her own life

                    war is ugly

it's also sad   the way brother killed brother   during

the Civil War   the way Grandpa Eli came to love

his brothers from the trenches   maybe even more

than his own family

                    how he stayed silent   a lot of the time

listening to Vivaldi   which Grandma Miriam said he believed

was *a supremely civilized achievement*   maybe Eli would know

having seen so many of his brothers   *let go of the grass*

which in a book I once read   is how a girl describes death

and also stars as holes in the sky   where light peeks through

from the opposite side

                    of life

Stars

It's a mystery to me   why the ancient Greek queen Cassiopeia

has a constellation in the sky   and the goddess Penelope

doesn't   Penelope who waited twenty years for her husband

Odysseus to return   from the Trojan War   and all that time

stayed loyal and unmoved   by the 108 suitors   waiting to ask

for her hand   Penelope who spent evenings   weaving a burial

shroud for Odysseus's father, Laertes   so that she wouldn't

have to deal   with all those fawning suitors   she told them

she would choose one   when she was done   as each evening

for three whole years   Penelope unwove   the rows of spun

linen   and each day began again   until Odysseus finally

came home
                I don't know   how that kind of brilliance

doesn't deserve at least a star   especially in light of Queen

Cassiopeia   who was always bragging   about her beauty

to the point where   Poseidon threatened to ruin her land

so that her husband   in trying to save it   agreed

to sacrifice their daughter Andromeda   by chaining her

to a rock   which is messed up   when you think who

gets what when it comes to stuff   like luck and constellations

the myth says the king and queen   were banished to the sky

which is why Cassiopeia   has a crooked line of stars in her name

but that's no punishment   like being burned at the stake

which is what they did to women   in Salem, Massachusetts

during the 1600s
                    I guess real life

is sometimes harsher than myth   I am not sure what

humans are supposed to learn from this   except maybe

not to brag   or that if you save yourself

or do what's right   people might not understand

Mary Janes

I am at Ray's   buying a dollar's worth of Mary Janes

which is twenty pieces   of peanut butter goodness in a bag

which I plan on eating   until my teeth ache   when Marta

bursts into the place   breathing hard saying

Alma! Alma!

Maureen's abuelo *is dead!*   a second later   she and I are

running hand in hand   across First Avenue and down

St. Marks until we reach our block   where we see

Maureen sitting on my stoop   her head on her knees

her glasses at her feet

Maureen! we are screaming

What happened?

What Happened

Doesn't feel very clear   except that Maureen's grandfather had

cancer all over his body   which likely began in his lungs

and drifted slowly as smoke unnoticed   to the rest of his

organs
            in the end they said

it might have been his heart   that gave out   from working

so hard   just to stay alive
                                   when Maureen's aunt arrives

two days later   it's a relief to see   her grandmother get out

of bed   begin tending to everything   that needs her attention

like Maureen   and the arrangements
                                       but when Maureen

comes rushing down the block   to tell us they've given her

a box   so she can pack her things   Clarissa drops her

Jolly Rancher   I let scatter my handful of jacks   and Marta

and Faith   come running fast   so we can all gather

around Maureen and cry   into each other's shoulders

Ohio   Maureen keeps saying   over and over   *Ohio* we keep saying *is not that far*   but the truth is

none of us   really knows exactly   where Ohio is

                                  or how to get there

Faraway

Even a place like Ohio   doesn't seem far enough   when

it comes to my parents   arguing in our apartment

over what it means   *to do your fair share*   of whatever

there is that needs doing
                                        like the dirty plates and cups

piled up in the sink   that my dad was supposed to wash

before his shift   so my mom wouldn't have   *to come*

home to it   or what about the fresh shirt   Dad thought

Mom had ironed for his interview   before she headed out

to work
                    ships in the night   my mom sometimes says

meaning she and Dad   barely see each other at all

and yet they still manage   to call one another

inconsiderate or *hypercritical*   every chance they get

making life with them a trip   on rough waters   where

like boats   traveling toward opposite shores   they're always

on the verge of colliding   where standing starboard

on my own personal craft   I grow tired of playing lookout
                                        of not being able to act

Jobs

My mom says my dad   is *always in the same boat*

still driving   still interviewing   for lame jobs

he doesn't want   would never even do   but has

to follow up on   because *the interview is a favor Mom's*

friend set up   blah blah blah   which is how Dad says it feels

not just the *blah* part   but the *setup* because how can his

heart be in it   when they're asking him   to shuffle papers

at a desk all day?
                    Well I say

rummaging the kitchen drawer   for fresh batteries   to put

in my Walkman   *Grandma Miriam would have told you*

to follow your heart
                        True my dad replies

barely disguising a grimace   because we both get

how corny it sounds   how it makes us cringe and laugh

even if it is good advice
                            my dad smooths his hair

sighs *Miriam was right, though, kiddo   But your mom*

thinks it's unfair   That you work nights? I ask

Yes he says   *And I get it   I just can't seem to find*

the kind of work I want
                              Like what?

Traveling the world? I smile   *Exactly* my dad nods

then begins shaking his head   as if just remembering

what a bad idea that is   *I can help out more* I propose

ejecting a tape   from my cassette deck   winding it with

my pinkie   *You know, help cook and stuff?*
                                        What? No!

my dad says   *It's not that   And you have your own chores*

and school   Besides, it's not your job to . . .   he pauses to stare

at the ceiling   *To what?* I ask   *To fix what's going on* he says

Drive

When I think of the word *drive*   I don't think of *ambition*

which as I learned   the other day in Ms. Foster's class   is also

one of its meanings   when I think of *drive*   I think of my dad

in his cab   and I think of myself   flying down our block

on my bike

        half standing leaning into the breeze

to pick up speed   while I whip around the corner   I also

think of the word   as a verb   in the past   and expressions

with *driven*   such as:

    insane

        up the wall

          away

            underground

              to drink

                snow

like in the phrase   *pure as the driven snow*   which actually

means not so pure at all

        a saying that must have been

born in New York   where snow falling softly on sidewalks

creates a hush of sparkling crystals   that muffle the noise

of the city   so that even our block   looks peaceful

and pretty until the snow   gets driven on   spun gray

by tires into dingy slush   before hardening into ice

that stays until spring

                  when I think of *driven*

I think of *ambition*   which my mom says   my dad doesn't

have because he *drives* all night   but is not *driven*   how

my own ambition   is about my vision   of where I want

my life to lead   how I'm going to get there   who I'm going

to be

            I feel too young   to have a vision so soon

but my mom says   *life sneaks up on you*   that it's never

too early to start   that you must lead with your heart

to find and follow your passion   so I've been riding

around on my bike   en*vision*ing myself   as an artist like

Andy Warhol   who became famous and rich   or a writer

like S. E. Hinton   who wrote *Rumble Fish*   or Quentin Crisp

without the makeup and the scarves

                        but it's hard

to picture myself   in the future   as I pedal down

our block   I picture my dad   just starting his shift

and wonder   when his vision left him

Janus

Was the ancient Roman god with two faces   not because

he lied a lot   or acted fake   but because he was the god

of gates and doorways   who looked both   back at the past

and toward the future   presiding over beginnings

and transitions   especially in conflict   Janus was

therefore   the god of war and peace   says Ms. Foster

and it seems serendipitous   because today after lunch

I got my period for the very first time   I was surprised

and a little queasy   even though I knew what it was   I have

never seen my own blood   except on a cut   which usually

gets cleaned and covered up right away   with no promise

to return in a month   for years to come   for the rest of most

of my life
                  so I made

a small pillow out of toilet paper   put it inside my underwear

I didn't want to see the nurse   and end up being late

for Ms. Foster   plus I didn't have a quarter   for the sanitary

napkin machine   which is always broken anyway   anyway

when my mom   comes home from work   I tell her about

Janus the god of transitions   she listens with interest

as she sautés   bok choy and ginger in her wok

when I tell her   about my period   she smiles

places her cigarette   on the edge of the stove   goes to find

me pads in the bathroom

                                        This means you can get pregnant

she says giving me the box   and a kiss on the forehead

I know I know I say

                            that night   as I'm getting into bed

I glimpse my face   in the mirror above my dresser

for a second I see two faces   or two minds or maybe

just mine with a faint trace   of the passage of time

whatever it is   I look and feel a little different

Oh, Snap!

Oh, snap! says Marta   when I tell her   *Oh, snap is right* I say

Did your mom slap you? Marta asks   *What? No!* I wave

my hand   *Well, my grandmother slapped my mother*

when she got her period   *Told my mom to get used to it*

because it hurts to be a woman sometimes

                                        Wow I say

that's cold   *Maybe* says Marta   *but it's the truth*

Sure as Maureen's in Ohio right now   *Yeah* I sigh

smoothing my ponytail   *I know I know*

Coney Island

My dad takes me to Coney Island   to *celebrate* my period

which is awkward at first   but I go with it

                                           we hit

the Cyclone   possibly the world's oldest roller coaster

with its rickety wooden rails and rattling track   they repaired it

a while back   but the scariest part is still the thought   that it

could splinter at any second   from the pitch of our screams

between ice cream and candied apples   and the centrifugal

force machine   with the dropping floor   I've almost

forgotten that   my dad has been staying   at Uncle Aaron's

house for the past few days   since he and my mom needed

a break

                as if like Faith's parents   to recover from a *bender*

only the emotional kind   it isn't the first time   and it won't be

the last   but something does seem changed   how, I can't say

but the way my dad   keeps squeezing my hand saying

Love you, kiddo   the vague sadness in his eyes   makes me

realize

                that growing up   doesn't always make life easier

Overthinker

Why do you overthink everything?   Miguel wants to know

What do you mean? I ask   as we scale the stairs

to his apartment
                        Like how you're always wondering

about dreams and what they mean   *And how you get*

so serious   *just because I don't like* Little House

Miguel unlocks the door   swings it open onto Churro

his bulldog   who comes lumbering   from behind

giant leaves   dragging a line of drool
                            I love coming here

after school   because Miguel's living room   is the closest thing

I've seen to a rain forest   with floor-to-ceiling   potted

palms and orchid plants   wicker chairs and tables in between

and mirrors that reflect the green   so the fronds seem

even deeper
                Miguel claims his parents can

only stand   the jungle of New York   if they have a jungle

of their own   one that reminds them of home   they jokingly

call it *Little Havana*   we're sitting under a small banana tree sharing some Twix when I say

I may be an overthinker

but have you ever thought that   maybe you don't think enough?

Yeah, actually I have   Miguel says closing his eyes

but I think more than you realize   especially now

List for Ms. Nola: Things
I Am Grateful For

My friends

My mom

My dad

Grandma Miriam

Books

My Walkman

Candy

My bike

Miguel

Rock on a Hill

My work is never done   Grandma Miriam used to say

until it was   until she wasn't darning socks   while

watching *One Life to Live*   until she could no longer make

the terrible meat loaf   everyone pretended to love

this is what I am thinking of   when Ms. Foster calls on me

so I say

Sisyphus is like my grandma Miriam

a couple of kids   in the back of the class   bust out laughing

Hold on   she gestures at them   *Go ahead, Alma*   *Well* I start

quickly smoothing my ponytail   clearing my throat

My grandma Miriam   didn't have to push a rock up a hill

She wasn't being punished by Zeus   but in a way she was

being punished   How so? Ms. Foster wants to know

Well I say   *she spent her whole life   cooking and cleaning*

for everyone else and every day   everything got eaten or dirty

again   Her rock rolling back down the hill   was that

she always had to start over   like Sisyphus and the "fruitless

labor"   you were talking about   It's like she was trapped by . . .

I pause for a moment to find the words   Ms. Foster tilts

her voice *By what?*   *I don't know* I say   *I guess by being*

a woman?

        Is that a question or a statement?

Ms. Foster wants to know   raising her eyebrows

It's a statement   I say slowly   trying to sound certain

It certainly is Ms. Foster smiles

Free

I don't know why   I feel so free sometimes   speeding

down the street   on my banana seat   the white tassels

on my handlebars   splayed like feathers   in the wind

this doesn't happen most days   but when it does

I could cruise around   my neighborhood for hours

my places and my people   just a blur   as I circle

Tompkins Square   or St. Mark's Church   my ponytail

whipping behind me   free to be me   going anywhere

I want to be

Once

Once I was riding my bike   down Third Avenue

eating a sandwich   listening to my Walkman

when my dad drove by   in his cab   which only ever

happened this one time   *For crying out loud, Alma!*

he honked   and shouted *Use your hands!*   I didn't

see him   didn't hear a thing   as he passed   with his fare

in the back

        the next morning

he told me the story   when I saw him   back at home

we laughed   because how funny   *But seriously, Alma*

he said   *That was crazy*

Free to Be You and Me

Is a book from the 1970s   that my mom gave me

when I was little   I used to listen   to the record

it came with   on the hooked rug   Grandma Miriam made

for us   and sing along to all the songs

like "It's All Right to Cry"

> *Crying gets the sad out of you*
> *It's all right to cry*
> *It might make you feel better*

and "Parents Are People"

> *People with children*
> *When parents were little*
> *They used to be kids*
> *Like all of you*
> *But then they grew*

I'd study each photograph   of children at the park   or kids

fishing or cooking   of parents painting   pushing strollers

or riding horses   I was looking I guess   for something

of myself in them   or the other way around   it's hard

to explain   what I took away   from all the time

I spent with that book   or how I found comfort

in the searching   for a feeling Ms. Foster   probably would have

connected to mythology   might have called *humanity*

The Waitress and the Swan

Sitting on the stoop   with my headphones on   but no music

in my ears   I can hear my own breathing   more clearly

even though our block   is kind of noisy   midmorning

with a delivery truck   parked on the corner   unloading

a pallet of washing machine parts   in front of

the Laundromat

                             I'm watching Clarissa

roller-skate in circles   until her mom says   she can cross

the street   to hang out with me   when a station wagon

pulls up   to the entrance of her building   it's brown like

the one they had on *The Brady Bunch*   and about as old

we'd been told that the waitress   on the fourth floor

is set to move out   so when I see a young man   at the wheel

with the same long reddish hair   I think he must be

her brother   come to take his sister home

                                       she appears

in the doorway   hoisting a large army duffel   looking pale

in the harsh light of this overcast morning   her posture

straight as a ballerina's   even saddled with a heavy load

making me think of *Swan Lake*   which is a ballet that I have

never seen but have heard of   and reminds me of the myth

"Leda and the Swan"

where Zeus turns himself into a bird

so he can have sex   with a mortal woman   named Leda

why she would want to be   with a swan makes no sense

to me   but I didn't raise my hand in class   to ask in case

there was something   about the sex   I was missing

plus the painting   Ms. Foster showed us   didn't help me

understand any better   why it's okay for a man   just

because he's a god   disguised as a swan   to get on top

of Leda   when she looks as shy or asleep   as she does

in the painting

I'm watching

the waitress hug her brother   their red hair blending

together on their shoulders   even from across the street

I can see the tenderness   between them

I want to tell

the girl in my class   who said *At least Leda gave birth to Helen   the most beautiful woman in the world*

that beauty means nothing   if it comes from

something ugly   that the Greeks blamed Helen's beauty

for the Trojan War   but Paris and Agamemnon   just used

Helen as an excuse   to do what they wanted to   that they

would have found

a reason to fight anyway

Check-In with Ms. Nola

Ms. Nola smells like coffee and roses   as she shows me

to the chair in her office   then closing the door   sings *Alma*

Alma Alma   smiling she says   *What's going on, honey?*

Nothing much   I mumble   kind of slumping down

in my seat   I'm really not into being here   right now

but I have nowhere else to be
                                    I like Ms. Nola

I don't want to be rude   but I am kind of annoyed

that she's so filled with positivity   when I'm in a cranky

mood   tired from listening to teachers   for the past

two hours   to my parents quiet-fighting   last night

in the other room
                        plus still kind of pissed

about having to be supersilent   during breakfast this morning

trying not to crunch   my superloud Kix   since I was

the only one up   until it was time for me to leave   Ms. Nola keeps

trying to break my silence with jokes   but she can see I am

out of sorts   that I'm not going to talk   no matter how sunny she is

> *All right, Miss Alma*

Ms. Nola sighs lightly after a while   *Let's end early today*

but how about you try writing down   what's going on?

Put it in a letter to me?

> *Great* I think *Homework*

Postcard from Ohio

Yesterday a postcard arrived   in the mail

from Maureen   it was addressed to me

but is for all of us:

3/5/82

Dear Alma, Marta, Clarissa, and Faith!

How are you? I miss you guys! Ohio is the greatest place ever!
We live in a trailer with my aunt and my two cousins
and there's grass all around and a lake nearby. And I
started at a new school. It's okay. I don't have many friends
yet but we get to play on a field during recess. So, that's cool.
Write me soon. I miss you guys. Grandma says hi.

        Love,
        Maureen

On the postcard is a twenty-cent   Black Heritage stamp

featuring Jackie Robinson   with a close-up of his face

and a little picture of him   in the bottom right corner

sliding into home plate   the postmark says

PAINESVILLE, OH   which makes us laugh   the *pain* part

but we are relieved   to know Maureen is happy

and at the same time sad   that she's so far away

                                                        it's strange

to imagine her playing in grass   in water that's not a pool

filled with screaming friends   or at a school with kids

who know nothing   about her   or her grandfather

the bare light bulb   in their city kitchen   the abject

conditions Maureen lived in   before moving to Ohio

a place that suddenly seems fascinating   as the four

of us huddle around her postcard

WELCOME TO OHIO
THE BUCKEYE STATE

What's "buckeye" mean?   Clarissa asks   *It's the state tree*

Faith says pointing *See?*   there's also a red cardinal

and a red carnation   and a flag and a barn

Wow we whisper
                        So cool

Preparation

I've been trying to use kung fu at school   not the fighting part

but the mental practice   like believing that if you are nervous

it means you want to do a good job   so instead of freezing up

you need to discipline your mind   convert your nervous

energy into doing really well   on your big vocabulary test

because you didn't do so hot   on the "Leda and the Swan" quiz

even though you know that myth   like the back of your hand

but all stirred up   while you were taking it   you kept

smoothing your ponytail   and shaking your leg   like you

had to go to the bathroom   so you asked but Ms. Foster said

No   not because she thought   you would cheat   but

because that's the policy   and anyway   now you are trying

to prepare by listening   to "Complete Control" by the Clash

extremely loud on your Walkman

                              and it feels like it might

                              be working

Letter for Ms. Nola

March 30, 1982

Dear Grandma Miriam,

    This letter is supposed to be for Ms. Nola, the counselor at my school, but I am writing to you because today I was looking at the book you gave me before you passed away. <u>A Woman of Independent Means</u> by Elizabeth Forsythe Hailey, in case you don't remember. But I think you do—or would—because even though you were very old, you still had a pretty good memory. You would always tell me about funny things I did when I was little or about things I said. You did call Dad and Uncle Aaron by each other's names sometimes, but that's totally understandable because they look so much alike—even if Uncle Aaron is a banker.

    What I noticed is that <u>A Woman of Independent Means</u> is a whole book made up of letters written by the main character. It's an epistolary novel. I just learned the term "epistolary." It was one of the more difficult words on my vocabulary test last week. You would be pleased to know I got a 92. Mental kung fu! I will explain more about that later.

    A lot has happened since you've been gone. For example, now I go to middle school—the one near my elementary school on Greenwich Avenue—which means I have a twenty-minute walk, instead of just turning the corner and walking three blocks. My favorite subject is English, but I also like art. I still love to read, but have been mostly reading mythology for my class with Ms. Foster—who is very demanding but also smart and fair, which makes me want to do the work.

A couple of years ago, we moved from the West Village to the East Village, and then moved again, farther down the block to a larger apartment. I have my own room now. It's small, but it's mine. Mom put a flower box of pansies on the fire escape to keep the pigeons from roosting right outside my window. You would be surprised to find how loud pigeons can be! Sometimes they would wake me before the sun was even up. Louder than the garbage trucks!

Our block is not so hot, though—kind of dirty and sketchy. I don't think you would be very happy about us living here. I do think you would like my friends, though. I still hang with Jennifer S. and Tara, who you met when we were in the third-grade play. Our new block has a bunch of kids and we travel as a crew—which means like a gang, not the bad kind, but the type that feels like family without the strife.

So far, being thirteen is a lot like mythology—by which I mean kind of complicated and a little confusing, with a bunch of crazy characters, some drama, and maybe some lessons for us mortals to understand. I am happy there's no test. But I guess life is the test—which, now that I write it, sounds heavy. Because unless you believe in reincarnation— which maybe I do—there's no unexcused absences or taking it over. It's like that soap opera you used to watch, One Life to Live.

There are these girls on our block that all the grown-ups call "the Girls." Some of them are only a little older than me, but they do things for money that we're not even supposed to be doing yet. And they go with grown men. And look sad and empty and skinny like cats that no one has fed—like they missed out on some of the lessons they were supposed to get when they were young. Or like something else went wrong. I look away from the doorways where they stand and try to focus on the street when I pass. It's not because I think what they have is catching, but more because I feel embarrassed. I don't know why.

Also, you might like to know that I am officially a woman—or technically or biologically or whatever . . . Meaning: I got my period! Which is supposed to be an important rite of passage, but is actually kind of a drag.

My mom told me that now I can get pregnant—which obviously I knew, but which also feels kind of freaky, because imagining myself with a baby is scary. Every year, the seniors at Alisha's high school have to carry an egg around in a basket for a week and pretend that it's a baby. If you ask me, that's a crazy way to prepare people for parenthood, because it's very difficult to get emotional about an egg. Only four kids in the class passed, which means a lot of broken babies. One boy put his egg in his gym bag and just left it in his locker. Maybe he will make a bad dad, but just because you don't take care of an egg doesn't mean you can't be a good parent one day. I don't know. The whole thing seems like a big waste of food. The arts high school I am going to in the fall doesn't make you do that, but I do have to take the subway all the way uptown. So, that will be new.

I wish you were here. I would ask if you remember trying to help me make Raggedy Ann's eyes look more like mine. Do you remember finding that old liquid eyeliner? And painting thick slanted lines like triangles at the corners, trying to make her button eyes look more almond? It was so funny when we realized that she looked more punk rock than half-Chinese, that with her orange hair we could never make her look like me.

"It takes all kinds," I remember you said. And that went for hair and eyes and boobs and thighs. I remember laughing really hard when you said "boobs and thighs." I miss you every day.

Love,
Alma

Lemonheads

We're leaning against the gate   in front of Faith's place

eating sno-cones   when we see something   we've

never seen before   it's hard to grasp at first   the way

Dario looks drunk   as he slow-stumbles   down

our block   followed closely by his older brother

who keeps pushing   the back of Dario's head   as we

watch from   the other side of the street   mouths open

red veins of cherry juice   winding down our arms

Dario lurches forward so hard   he almost falls face-first

onto the pavement   that's when Miguel calls out

Hey, yo

             Christian, why you got to—   before Miguel

can finish his question   Christian whips around

and sneers   then smacks the box of Lemonheads fast

from Dario's hand   we all watch the yellow candies

bounce like beads   around their feet and skitter

across the sidewalk

             a sound of teeth

but slow motion   as if the whole street is silent   except

for Maria's soft crying   *Dios mío* under her breath

Faith puts on her headphones
                                              but my gaze

stays fixed on Christian   my whole body tense   as Miguel's

fists stay clenched   until the brother   reaches the corner

where Dario's eyes flash back at us   from over his shoulder

as Christian gives his head a final shove   I see for the very

first time   that Dario has beautiful eyes   dark and wide

even when he's trying not to cry

Preparation

My mom used to send me to the store   with a five-dollar bill

to buy a box of Tampax   and a pack of Marlboro cigarettes

I was eleven   didn't have my period yet   she knew it made me

feel uptight   to ask for the tampons   kept on the shelf

behind the counter   in plain sight   with the lottery tickets

and the condoms   but she also knew I wouldn't refuse

If Ray asks she'd add   *tell him it's the blue pack*   nonchalant

as if she wasn't aware   it made me uncomfortable

                          it's not that

my mom didn't care   but like lighting the oven   she wanted

me to learn by doing

            I had to be prepared

Back in Black

All I can find   is a red Coca-Cola T-shirt   but to enter

Great-grandmother's room   and offer her the customary

plate of oranges   I must change

our whole relationship

is based on this   me wearing red for good luck   her smiling

and nodding   us presenting each other food   Great-

grandmother usually has sweets   already laid out for me

a plate piled high   with black bean cakes   egg tarts

and Almond Roca   which is a fancy kind of American

chocolate   that only Chinese people seem to eat   Great-

grandmother is tiny and beautiful   with the face of an old

woman and the eyes of a young girl   she parts her black-

gray hair with two bobby pins   so that it frames her

features at the chin   wears a brown silk jacket and slippers

no matter where she is going   or where she is

which is

mostly home   she hasn't left Chinatown since 1974

when my grandmother   took her to Macy's   for a winter coat she never wore

    lately Great-grandmother

has grown so frail that when she wants to leave

the apartment Grandfather has to carry her down three

flights of stairs to the entrance of the building where

she's content to spend her time in a folding chair

watching the people pass by

        when she offers me

a bean cake I take it with both hands bow slightly

then we sit and smile at each other for a while with

genuine affection but in silence since she doesn't speak

English and I barely speak Chinese "Back in Black"

by AC/DC is playing on the radio that Great-grandmother always

has on in the other room nodding her head she softly

hums the tune *Good song* I say holding up my thumb

she gives me a thumbs-up back and we laugh

Mary Jane

Is another word for marijuana   what Tara calls it   as she pulls

a plastic bag   out of the vegetable bin   in her mother's

boyfriend's fridge

we're at his house after school

with Jennifer S. and Josh   and another kid I just met

who lives in Josh's building   on Fifth Avenue   Tara has the keys

to her mother's boyfriend's place   because they are in a serious

relationship   Tara says and Greg wants her   *to feel like*

he's family   even though he and her mom aren't married

have only been dating three months   Tara doesn't like Greg

very much   but she likes to go through his stuff   so here

we are   in his living room eating Doritos   as Jennifer S.

holds the bag up to the light   *Isn't he going to be pissed?* I ask

because I've actually never done this   I'm thinking how weird

it is   that even though we're surrounded by them   no one

on my block does drugs   except for the adults   and Miguel's

old babysitter   who smoked weed laced with PCP

a chemical that makes you crazy   and ended up in the psych ward at St. Vincent's which   I don't think she ever

really left

               Josh plops down on the couch

next to me   but I'm focused on the picture   in my mind

of my mom crying   or me on a stretcher   outside St. Vincent's

or standing in a doorway   with a bruise on my eye   a man

driving by   watching me from his car

                             Nah   Josh laughs

Greg doesn't care   *but we don't smoke Greg's weed*

Too weak he snorts   and gestures with his chin   to the kid

from his building   who flashes him two fingers   in a *V*

as a sign of peace   Tara and Jennifer S. meanwhile   are jumping

on Greg's bed   screaming at MTV   where David Bowie

is singing "Fashion"

      There's a brand-new dance but I don't know its name
      That people from bad homes do again and again

He's so gay   says the kid from Josh's building   *Gay-mazing!*

Josh shouts   we all laugh   only they laugh much harder

                    long after the song is over

Ronald Reagan

Means nothing to me   he's the president of the United States

but when I look at his face   I don't see a way in   I'm telling

Ms. Nola this   as I am sitting in her office   staring at a bowl

of pins on her desk   that read JUST SAY NO   *To what?* I ask

already I'm making a list in my head   of things I would refuse

To drugs she says   *It's Mrs. Reagan   the first lady's campaign*

Um, okay I laugh   *Yeah* Ms. Nola smiles   like she knows

it's futile to stop drugs   with a bunch of buttons

That's futile I say   *Good word* she says   *It was on my vocab*

test I add   *It means hopeless   Indeed* Ms. Nola laughs *Indeed*

So, what's up with Ronald Reagan?   Ms. Nola wants to know

Nothing I say   *I just think we should have a president   who*

doesn't look that way   What way? she asks   *Like he's smiling*

but not listening   Like he couldn't care less   about what

you think or say   Like Mr. Gordon, how he's always droning on

all self-important   never even stopping to listen   just telling us

not to do drugs or whatever   without even knowing what

it means if we do

Ms. Nola nods as I go on

Because some people can do drugs   and just go straight

to college and then live in fancy apartments   But some

people end up standing in doorways   for the rest of their

lives and maybe even die there

                              I hear you, honey

Ms. Nola replies   *I think I know what you're trying to say*

Good I'm practically shouting again   so I stop and take

a deep breath   the way Ms. Nola once showed me

smoothing my ponytail

                              I say to myself *Alma, get a grip*

Grip

Dario is back on our block   trying to hock an old G.I. Joe

action figure   for $1.50   so he can see *Death Wish II*

on St. Marks Place   Clarissa and I wave him off

like *That's sad*
                we turn and go back

to trading Now and Later flavors   *I'll give you two banana*

for one watermelon Clarissa proposes   *No way* I say

I hate banana   How about blue raspberry?
                                    Dario breaks in

again   *It's the G.I. Joe with Kung Fu Grip   Kung fu what?* I ask

Grip says Dario   trying to give us a demonstration   but the arm

is broken
            Looks like he's thumb-wrestling I snort

I'll give you two bucks   for your bike, though says Clarissa

Man of Action Dario continues   *That's wack* I laugh   but when

Dario wheels around   stares off in the distance like *Damn*

I can see   he really wants to go to the movies
                                    Here I say

handing him two quarters   *Whaaat?* Clarissa whines

in protest   I smooth my ponytail   quick give her a look

like *Come on*   *Hey, yo* she says   *Here's another quarter*

Now get lost! we both shout   Dario sees we're joking

smiles as he rides off   *That boy needs a new bike*

we say   *I mean, look at his legs   Sad*

Time

Faith and I are on the roof again   wrapped up in our tubes

sharing a giant bag of Twizzlers   tonight, though   we're

not on the lookout for aliens   we figure they'll find us

if they want to plus   sometimes a person gets tired

of waiting
                    for the thing they want to happen

to happen   so we're just enjoying the cool night air

having random conversations about life   the way you can

when you feel relaxed with a friend   not particularly stressed

able to notice how the Con Ed Building   looks magically lit

with a warm glow   shining from between the little pillars

of the tower   how it doesn't matter   as much as it usually does

that the clock   facing your block is still broken   the way

it bothers you on other days   that the ones pointing north

and west are always correct   as if time were a sign

of respect
                    I was eight when Grandma Miriam told me

Love is time spent   But you spend a lot of time folding clothes

I said   *And I know you don't love that*   tonight, though

I understand   more of what she meant   unlike the stars

and endless lights   that dot the sky   people only get a certain

amount of time   Grandma Miriam had seventy-six years

what will I do with mine?

Night and Day

Dad is back from Uncle Aaron's   he's decided to stop

driving nights   says he'll stick to day shifts   the way

office people punch in   at nine and leave at five   have normal

lives where everyone is home   awake at the same time

he'll have to work six days   instead of four nights   to make

the same money   but he thinks that's better for us   as a family

truthfully
         I am not convinced   as my dad is explaining this

he and my mom are sitting up   in their rumpled bed

tired from another night of quiet-fighting   I can practically

see the dark cloud   hovering over their heads   the air

heavy around them   laced with cigarette smoke

and regret
         my throat closes around the words

That won't change a thing   I can see they are trying to be

optimistic   so I say *Great*   *I have to go or else I'll be late*

Space Invaders

Clarissa and Alisha   are the only ones who have Atari

which means   when it's too hot or cold outside   everyone

spends a lot of time   piled on their leather couch   playing

Space Invaders
                        which is addictive   but kind of boring

if you stop to think about it   which you don't   all jacked up

on Jolly Ranchers or pickle juice   while you wait your turn

to blast your laser cannon   at the boxy green aliens   raining

down from space
                        Bonus ship! Miguel shouts at Faith

as we root for her elimination   so we can battle each other

I suck at *Space Invaders*   because I'm not committed

truth is if Atari didn't exist   I'd be just as happy   doing

something else   but Clarissa and Alisha   live for this

begged their parents for a year   even chipped in to get

the system
                        Miguel and I are sitting

on the couch   I am aware that my thighs   are sticking

to the leather   making funny sounds   I'm in cutoffs

because even though   it's only May   it's ninety degrees outside

but I'm really sweating
                                because Miguel is holding

my hand for the first time ever   I am okay with this

surprised by how it feels more private   than a kiss

but as he moves his hand   to the top of my thigh   my heart

starts racing   I feel warm inside with an urge   to jump up

and run away   instead I take a deep breath   lean into him

and say *Miguel, you're invading my space*

Dream

So, what do you think this one means?   I ask my dad

as he struggles   to brew a cup of coffee   he's up early

to drive for the second day in a row   and it's not going

very well   he looks pained   scooping the beans into

the grinder   squeezing his eyes shut   bracing for

the high-pitched whir of the mill   *Give me a sec* he says

Just have to make the . . .   his voices trails off   as he

pulls milk from the fridge   *Okay* he says   rubbing

his eyes   *Shoot!*

                     Okay I say   *I'm on the D train going*

to Brooklyn to see Grandma Miriam   *only I don't really*

know which stop to get off at   *and I am alone*

                                Actually

my dad cuts in   *It's the B*

                    Be what? I ask

B train to Kings Plaza he yawns   *Yeah, okay* I say   *Anyway,*

I'm on the B train   *holding a box of letters*   *full of very*

important secrets   *but I am not allowed to know*   *what they*

are and it's up to me to protect them
                                        taking a big slurp

of coffee   my dad jabs his finger at the air   *What?* I ask

Actually he adds   *It may also be the Q   I think now*

you have to transfer to the Q train   Or is that only when

there's track work?   What? I huff   *I don't know!*

Hello, can I finish here?   Sure, sorry he says

So, I have to guard these secrets   and there's all these

creepy people on the train   who want to steal

the letters from me   and I have to get to Grandma

Miriam's   because she has this special safe

with an unbreakable kryptonite lock   pouring more

coffee into his mug   my dad says   *Okay, stop*

Stop what? I ask
                  Boys he laughs

Boys, what? I want to know   *The dream is about boys*

Oh my god, again? I shout   *Well, you asked*

he mumbles   grinning into his cup   I feel mad

but I'm trying not to smile   *Not everything is about boys,*

you know I grumble   *True* my dad agrees   wiping his

glasses on his sleeve   *But this one is*   *Love you, kiddo*

he says   toasts me with his coffee

                                        Argh I huff *Love you too*

Pandora's Box

Pandora's Box :
a prolific source of troubles

Ronald Reagan is flashing   his empty smile at me

from the bulletin board   in Mr. Richter's study hall

where I am writing down   the rest of my dream

on loose-leaf   so I don't forget the part   about finally

getting to Grandma Miriam's   only to realize I don't have

a key to the kryptonite lock   for the safe on the floor

in her bedroom closet   where I sit

surrounded by shoes   the very important letters

on my lap   bundled and tied with white string   I am trying

not to be tempted   by the secrets they contain   so I fumble

with the lock instead   which is glowing green

hot to the touch
                    I flinch and suddenly

I am surrounded by sheets of papyrus   printed with fancy

cursive   a note that reads:

Faith's parents are alcoholics

another that says:

Divorce is imminent

NAME: Alma Rosen   **DATE:** May 3, 1982

IN-CLASS ASSIGNMENT: OUTLINE FOR FINAL ESSAY

TITLE: PANDORA: ALL ABOUT MISOGYNY*

*MISOGYNY (n.): a hatred of women

PARAGRAPH I:

INTRODUCTORY SENTENCE:

There are two versions of the creation of Pandora and both of them are terrible.

In one version of "Pandora's Box," Zeus, the king of the gods, is angry at Prometheus for giving fire to mankind and for saving man the best parts of the meat from animal sacrifices. Zeus creates Pandora to get revenge on Prometheus. She is a sweet and lovely thing to look upon, whose name means "gift of all." When Zeus's "beautiful disaster" is done, he introduces Pandora as "the first woman and the mother of all women, who are an evil to men, with a nature to do evil." The Greek gods wanted men to hate women and to think that they were evil—which is the real myth, if you ask me.

CONCLUDING SENTENCE:

This version of Pandora's creation is a lie.

EVIDENCE:

p. 88, Mythology, by Edith Hamilton

PARAGRAPH II:

INTRODUCTORY SENTENCE:

The other version of this creation myth isn't any better.

In the second story of Pandora, each Greek god puts something dangerous into a box. They give the box to Pandora and forbid her to open it. Then they give Pandora to Epimetheus, who happily accepts her, even though he has been told to never accept anything from Zeus. In this creation story, the source of Pandora's "wicked nature is her curiosity," because when Pandora opens the box, "out fly plagues innumerable, sorrow and mischief for mankind."

CONCLUDING SENTENCE:

This second story of creation is a good example of a double standard.

My grandma Miriam used to say, "What's good for the goose is good for the gander"—a goose being female, a gander being male—meaning things should be the same for men and women, which obviously they are not.

EVIDENCE:

p. 89, Mythology, by Edith Hamilton

PARAGRAPH III:

INTRODUCTORY SENTENCE:

The first creation story is misogynist.

In the first version, Zeus is teaching men to hate women even more than he hates man. By creating Pandora and giving her away like a gift, he is portraying her as something "precious and delicate" instead of as a person. And by making her "sweet and lovely to look at," Zeus is implying that men would only be interested in knowing Pandora if she is pretty, which is only true of some men and sets a bad example for all men. Plus it's insulting to call Pandora a "beautiful disaster" because a disaster is tragic and Pandora is curious, which is not a disaster or a tragedy.

CONCLUDING SENTENCE:

EVIDENCE:

PARAGRAPH IV:

INTRODUCTORY SENTENCE:

The second version is misogynist too.

(as if she is a box) (probably because she is pretty)

(interesting how Epimetheus doesn't get in trouble for not listening)

(curiosity is a crime for a woman but not for a man?)

CONCLUDING SENTENCE:

EVIDENCE:

PARAGRAPH V:

INTRODUCTORY SENTENCE:

Mythology is misogynist.

CONCLUDING SENTENCE:

EVIDENCE:

Open your eyes.

Dear Ms. Foster:

I need more time.

Yours truly,

Alma

Thesaurus

It's Saturday morning   I am sitting on my stoop   listening

to the Pretenders   flipping through my mother's

old thesaurus from Catholic school   when Dario rolls up

on his tiny bike   all like *What's up?*   *Why are you out*

so early?   *What are you doing out?* I ask   *I'm always up*

early he answers   *Everyone else in my house sleeps late*

Same here I say

                    What book is that? Dario wants to know

It's the thesaurus   I hold it up   so he can see its faded

linen cover

               What's it about? he asks *Dinosaurs?*

No I laugh   *It's a book of synonyms*   *Cinnamon?*

Oh my god I snort   *Come here* I wave   shove over a little

on the step   *See* I say opening up   to the *A*'s

"Apparatus" is a noun   *its synonyms are*

> *machine*
>
> *machinery*
>
> *equipment*
>
> *instruments*

Cool says Dario *I've seen one of these before*   *Try looking up*

"wack" we both laugh   *I don't think they had that back then* I say

But what about . . .   skipping to *F*   I run my finger

down the page and stop   on *female* and read aloud

> *female*
>
> *womankind*
>
> *womanhood*
>
> *femininity*
>
> *muliebrity*

Muli-what? Dario cuts in

> *fair sex*
>
> *weaker sex*

What the heck? I say   *Check this out!*   *Under "slang" it says*

> *femme*
>
> *frail*
>
> *dame*
>
> *skirt*
>
> *broad*
>
> *sister*
>
> *tomato*

Skirt? we shout   *Tomato?* Dario says shaking his head

When's this book from? he asks   *Um* I turn to the front *1962*

That's messed up he says   *I was right   It is a dinosaur*

That should be extinct he adds   pulling a Kit Kat from

his pocket   Dario smiles
                                    I'm gonna start

calling you Skirt   Don't you dare I hiss   giving him

an elbow to the ribs   *Nah* he says handing me a Twix

What's with all the candy? I ask   *I stole it from*

my brother   You know, the "weaker sex"   he laughs

and shakes his fist
                                    Total tomato I say

Smoking

Grandfather thinks   smoking is improper for a woman

maybe because   he does not watch TV   or look

at magazines   if he did   he might begin to believe

that smoking is a sign of freedom   from the way they

portray women on the go   holding cigarettes   but I

can see my mom is attached   to her pack-and-a-half

habit as much as any man   that the pull of nicotine

is a mini ball and chain   she hauls around in her purse

all day
                    she recently switched   from Marlboro Reds

which are worse than   her new Benson & Hedges

Ultra Lights which are superlong and skinny   like the model

in the ad   with the windblown hair   and briefcase in her hand

as if she's heading to an office   even though she looks

seventeen
                    my mom says they contain less nicotine

why she says she made the change   as she lights up

in Grandmother's kitchen   we're watching the Yankees game and pinching pork dumplings   until Grandfather comes in

tells my mom   all gruff   to leave his sight   if she wants

to smoke

                so downstairs she goes   Ultra Lights

and matches in her fist   to smoke in their doorway

next to the rancid garbage   from the vegetable stall

I know it makes my mom feel small   as she watches

the fishmonger sweep blood   into the street   to be

banished from her own parents' home   but she would

never let on

                smoking is the least she's done

to offend them   I should know   I am living proof

Letter to Maureen

May 12, 1982

Dear Maureen,

How are you? Everyone on the block misses you a lot. Even Dario—just kidding! Ohio looks cool. I hope you still love it. Almost done with 8th grade. On to high school! Crazy! You'll never guess who asked me out two weeks ago: Jason from my homeroom—the one I told you about with the big Afro and the Black Power pick stuck in it. I've been looking at that pick and the back of Jason's head for two years and he has never even said a word to me. He's fine, but mostly silent, so when he turned around the other day and said, "You want to hang out sometime?" I said hell no! But in a kind way, because what would we talk about?

Anyway, Miguel and I are still spending time together but I'm not sure if I'm that into it. I am ambivalent—feel like this is a time of transition for me. Nothing is happening, but a lot is happening. Maybe that doesn't make sense? In my English class, we learned about a Roman god named Janus—who is the god of gates and doorways, which are symbols of beginnings and endings. There's a statue in Rome where Janus has two faces—one young and one old. I have been thinking about this a lot. Sometimes I feel like I am about to open a door or walk through a gate and it makes me feel a little afraid and excited at the same time—like I don't know whether what I find on the other side will be terrible or really great. You walked through a door and it opened on Ohio, so I am hopeful. I have to go now and help my mom with the groceries, then over to Lisha and Carissa's to play Atari. I wonder what you are doing in Ohio right now. Something fun, I hope.

Love, Alma

P.S. Write back!

P.P.S. I got my period!!

Day and Night

You got me workin', workin' day and night

        —Michael Jackson, "Workin' Day and Night"

We're at Tara's mother's   boyfriend Greg's house again

making a mess of his record collection   while Josh and the kid

from his building   whose name turns out is also Josh

are riffling through   a stack of *Mad* magazines   on the coffee

table   making a mess of things   flicking Skittles at the fire-

place but mostly missing

                        I am thinking   this would not

be okay with Greg   but no one seems   to care what Greg

would think   so I go to the pantry   to find some chips

figuring he won't miss them   when I get back from

the kitchen   Tara and Jennifer S. have laid out   several

album covers in a row   *I don't know* Tara says   *In this one*

he looks fine   pointing to Michael Jackson's face

on the cover of *Off the Wall*   *Yeah* says Jennifer S.

That was 1979   *But now look* she goes

                                    holding up

the sleeve of this year's release   *On* Thriller *his nose*

looks totally different she says   *It does* I agree

spraying potato chips as I say it   *That's messed up*

I continue
                    Ew Tara laughs

waving off the shower of crumbs   *Sorry* I spray   *But*

he does look a little whiter   Tara says then turning to me

What's that about?   *What do you mean?* I crunch

Why are you asking me?   *Well* she pauses   *You're half-*

Chinese   *Do you ever want to look more white?*   *No way* I say

Actually, some Chinese people think I'm lucky   *because my eyes*

are wider   *Wow, really?* Jennifer S. shouts   over the music

I know I shake my head   Tara sighs *I guess Chinese people*

are just as nuts as everyone else
                                    Like what is that?

asks Jennifer S.   *Hating yourself?*   the two Joshes nod

their heads   from across the room   but it's hard to tell

if they're agreeing with us   or just grooving to the music

either way it feels messed up

Return to Sender

My most recent letter to Maureen   showed up in our mailbox

this morning   with RETURN TO SENDER   stamped

in red ink across the envelope

                              plus an old-fashioned-looking

picture of a finger   pointing nowhere   like the "Go to Jail"

kind you'd find   in a game of Monopoly   below it was

a list that read

> ☐ *MOVED LEFT NO ADDRESS*
> ☐ *NO SUCH NUMBER*
> ☐ *MOVED NOT FORWARDABLE*
> ☐ *ADDRESSEE UNKNOWN*

none of the boxes   were checked, though   so I wasn't

sure what the issue was   I asked my mom   what she

thought was going on   *I mean, look* I said   *The address*

I wrote is correct   I held up the postcard   Maureen

first sent as evidence   *I don't know what to tell you, honey*

my mom shook her head   from the way she worried

the rings on her left hand   with the fingers of her right

I could tell   whatever she was thinking   was not good

Black Is Beautiful

I want to thank you   *for that letter*   *to your grandma Miriam*

Ms. Nola is saying   but I'm looking past her   at the BLACK

IS BEAUTIFUL poster   taped up behind the dead fern

in the dusty macramé holder   hanging from the ceiling

So, what's going on?   she wants to know   following

my eyes   turning to look over her shoulder

toward the poster   *Two things* I say

First: When did you get that poster?

Two: Your plant really needs water

Yes   Ms. Nola laughs   *It certainly does*

I have a black thumb   *I can never keep plants alive*

That's weird I say   *Why's that?* she asks

One: Because you're a giving type of person

like you kind of keep kids alive by talking to them

Two: "Black thumb" sounds kind of racist

Well she smiles   *Helping is my job*   *and "black thumb" is just*

an expression   *the opposite of having a green thumb*

in which a person is good   *at helping plants grow*

And black Ms. Nola adds   *is a color often associated*

with death   but I know what you mean   I don't see it as

a racial thing   at least the way I'm using it here

                                                    Okay I say

For Chinese people white is the color of death   Like if you give

someone white flowers   it's practically the same as saying

"I hope you die"   Extreme bad luck   And you always have

to wear red I add   *Well, not every day but on special occasions*

That's interesting Ms. Nola remarks   *I see you looking at*

my poster

                Yes I say   *Is it new? I've never seen it before*

No, it's been here   as long as I have   which is going on

nine years now she says   shaking her head and looking off

like *Wow, time flies*

                        Wow I say   *The baby in the picture*

is so cute   It would be great I add   *if they had posters*

like that for all kinds of people   I agree Ms. Nola says

I guess some people need them   more than others

That's true I nod   *Black Is Beautiful* I read aloud

I wonder if that baby believes it

                                    I hope so

Ms. Nola smiles   *Same here* I say

smoothing my ponytail

                    Same here

171

Warheads

Alisha and Clarissa's aunt   on their father's side   is visiting

for two months from Taiwan   which means we can't spend time

in the living room or play Atari   because she's taken over

the entire space   with her massive suitcases   filled with

designer clothes and makeup

                              it also means Warheads

which is a candy   you can't get in the United States   which

burns your mouth   with so much sugar acid   that you scream

out loud   as your eyes water up   and your nose begins to run

we love them   because they're fun   love Clarissa's aunt

for bringing this five-pound bag   of green-apple- and cherry-

flavored insanity into our lives

                              up on Faith's roof

a bunch of us are eating Warheads   by the handful until

the stomachaches kick in   until Miguel shows up in a bad

mood   obviously pissed that Dario is with us   because

since when?   he doesn't like that Dario's   not from

our block   but that fact doesn't seem   to matter much

to anyone else anymore

Marta hands Miguel a Warhead

says *Toma, prueba uno, está rico*   Miguel pops it into

his mouth   within seconds   his eyes are bugging out

we're all laughing   as he coughs and spits   bright

green juice   all over the roof   Dario goes over to slap

Miguel on the back   jokingly   as if he's saving him

when his fake Rolex watch   catches the chain of Miguel's

Jesus in Pain   rips it right off   with a fast snap of gold

flashing in the hot June sun

Faggot Miguel yells

pushing Dario down onto the tar   *Wait, what?*

Dario is saying   as Miguel plants a punch   right in his face

then turning and shaking his fist   scoops up his broken

necklace   and stomps down the stairs

What the hell?

we're all saying   *Dario, are you okay?*   he's fine but

Marta is crying   Clarissa and Faith have their arms

around her   I'm looking over the edge   of the roof

watching Miguel stalk back   to his building   the Jesus

head swinging   from his clenched hand   as he fumbles

in his pocket for his key

Cold

What? I grumble   waving the envelope at Clarissa   *You think*

Maureen's already moved?   *It doesn't make sense*   *She just*

got there
                    I don't know!   Clarissa says squishing

her Tootsie Roll wrapper   between her fingers

pinging it into the street   adding *Maybe her house*

burned down or something
                                   Don't do that! I say

What? Clarissa asks   *Litter* I reply   *Oh my god* Clarissa rolls

her eyes   *You and the littering thing!*   pointing, she continues

Look at that sidewalk!   *It's filled with trash*
                                              Doesn't matter

I shake my head   *You shouldn't make it worse*   *Plus you*

shouldn't say   stuff about people's houses burning down

It's bad luck
                    What? Clarissa snaps   *Now you're my mother?*

Yup I smile   *But seriously, what about Maureen?*

I don't know sighs Clarissa   *I mean, she was living in her aunt's*

trailer, right?   Yes I nod *with her cousins*   *You know* Clarissa pauses   *sometimes people just lose touch   It doesn't seem like*

you care that much I say   *I care* Clarissa protests   *I just mean*

it's not like there's anything we can do
                              I don't know about you

I say *but I promised I would write Maureen   and she promised*

she would write to me
                    So Clarissa says

Then maybe she'll write you back   with her new address

Or you could hire a private detective   Or you could just

forget about it
                    Jeez, Clarissa I shake my head

How'd you get so cold?   I don't know Clarissa laughs

                    Seriously, I don't know

Night and Day

You got me workin', workin' day and night

        —Michael Jackson, "Workin' Day and Night"

Nine-to-five   is not working   the way my parents had hoped

I myself could have told them that   but I guess they had

to learn it on their own

                          Mom's day is still Dad's night

and the other way around   meaning they haven't found

a way to get along   being home for dinner all week

doesn't make the difference   you might think

                                  over time

their loud fighting became quiet-fighting   and quiet-fighting

became choked silence   to the point   that I tried to wear

my Walkman at meals   so I didn't have to listen to the sounds

of chopsticks clicking   or forks scraping plates   everyone chewing

until their jaws ache

                    the first time

they let me keep my headphones on at dinner   I listened

to "Too Much Pressure" by The Selector   which was perfect as part of my mental kung fu   except my mom kept motioning for me to

not eat so fast   and my dad kept motioning at her

to *stop that*
                    I had to cut dinner short ride my bike

around the block ten times   keeping my eyes straight ahead

away from the doorways   in order to get a grip
                                      now

they only let me wear my Walkman at breakfast   because *Okay*

mental kung fu before school   but *antisocial* otherwise

I think *they* could use   some music therapy   because just

being awake at the same time   isn't the same as being

                      of one mind

The 411

I've checked our mailbox   every day this week   but there was

nothing in it for me   which isn't surprising   I usually only get

mail around my birthday
                              a Hallmark card

from Grandma Miriam   with *Granddaughter*   engraved

in fancy golden script   some sweet but schmaltzy verse

about how special I am   plus a five-dollar bill   slipped

into it   even if she always   had another gift to give me

anyway
                    today, though   I was really hoping for a letter

from Maureen   who lingers in the back of my mind   at times

when we're hanging out as a crew   or I'm biking to Ray's

and definitely every time I pass   her old apartment door

on my way up to Alisha and Clarissa's floor
                                                      but honestly

I think of Maureen   less and less each week

and it bothers me   that no one mentions her   very often

anymore
                    that a friend could be   so easy to forget

is upsetting   as if people will only remember you   if you have

a constellation in your name   or if you're rich and famous

I'm thinking this   as I dial 411   the information line

to see if I can find   a new address for Maureen   it's still

ringing when I realize   that I don't even know her aunt's

name   *Painesville, Ohio* is all I have to go on   and like

everything else   I think of   when it comes to Maureen

it's not enough   and never will be

Quits

Mom is in her pantyhose and bra   standing at the wok

stir-frying broccoli with ginger sauce   smoking a cigarette

when she tells me   that she's going to San Francisco

on a trip to see her friend from college   that she and Dad

are *calling it quits*   *Wait, what?* I go   pulling off

my headphones   *Calling it what?*   I say as I grab

the stepladder   sit down in silence   for a moment

by the stove   *You make it sound like   you're giving up*

smoking or something I snap   my voice small

and sharp like a splinter

                              It's not that we don't love

each other my mom sighs   tears forming in her eyes

It's just that we can't live together   *We think it's better*

this way, Alma   *I think you might even agree*   I see

my mom's hands shaking   as she tosses her cigarette

into the sink   places her spatula on the counter

and kneeling down by my seat   holds my face

looks into my eyes   for what feels like a long time

Why isn't Dad here?   my voice breaks   *We thought*

it would be better   *if we each spoke to you separately*

at first   *You always get so quiet*   *when it's the both of us*

He wants to talk to you   *He does*

                                   It doesn't surprise me

I cry   *but it's still messed up*   Yes Mom nods   casting off

a last thread of smoke   from around her head   *It is*

and we'll be sad for a while   *Even me and Dad*   *It takes time*

Time is important
                        I am thinking of Grandma Miriam

how she said   *Love is time spent*   only I don't think

she meant for it   to be separate
                                 I'm beginning to think

I don't know   what anything means anymore

Call It Quits

call it quits :
to stop doing something

Synonyms

abandon   break off   cease
conclude   discontinue   drop
give up   halt   leave   retire
suspend   terminate   withdraw
desist   end   resign   secede
call it a day   cut it out   get on the wagon
give notice   give over   hang it up
kick over   kick the habit   knock off
leave off   pack in   quit cold
sew up   surcease   take the cure
wind up   wrap up   what the?

Sign of the Twins

Yvonne and Yvette are at Ray's getting matching snacks:

two bags of Funyuns
two chocolate Yoo-hoos
two packs of grape Bubble Yum

they're dressed all in black today   like heat magnets

in the eighty-five-degree weather   black from their tank tops

to their track shorts   down to their matching skippies

plus all black accessories   including plastic headbands

rubber bracelets   and satin fanny packs slung around

their waists like disco holsters   for storing change

and gum and such
                          I'm standing behind them

a quarter sweating metallic in my palm   waiting to pay

for my bag of fried pork rinds   thinking it's as if

Yvonne and Yvette are a sign   symbols for how I feel

dark like something's died   right here in the middle of the day

in Ray's store   in the middle of my thirteen-year-old life

dark like a shadow at my shoulder   that makes breathing

even eating   kind of hard   which is how I felt

when Grandma Miriam died

                              though at nine years old

I didn't know   that things come and go   that as my mother

said *We must let them*

                    when Yvonne looks over

her shoulder at me   *Hey, you're part Puerto Rican, right?*

I feel like I'm about to cry   *Nah* says Yvette clicking her tongue

Alma?   She's Korean

                    Chinese I sigh *I'm half-Chinese*

Told you Yvonne says to Yvette   *Told me what?*

See, stupid Yvonne waves in my direction   *Now you made*

her sad   Yvonne flicks Yvette on the back   pushes past

some kids piling into the store   rattling the bells

on Ray's door

                    which ring loudly in my ears

while sounding far away   like underwater sirens

                    a quiet emergency

Emergency

Clarissa is wrestling   with a jumbo pack of Blow Pops

when Faith comes skating up   huffing lightly with a wad

of gum in her mouth   *So, what's up with this emergency*

meeting? she wants to know

                                Let's wait for Dario I say

watching Clarissa   give the plastic bag a final rip

spilling all thirty-six pops   onto the pavement

as if she's cracked a piñata   right there on the sidewalk

Oh, snap! Marta yells   and we all crouch down fast   to rescue

them

            Five-second rule I say   unwrapping mine

handing one to Faith   *I hate grape* she says   *Cherry then* I offer

her a cluster   hold it out like a tiny bouquet   she plucks one

smirks with a half curtsy   *Why, thank you, monsieur*

I think you mean "mademoiselle," actually I reply

Dario speeds by on his bike   and Clarissa starts waving

her arms like she's guiding a plane   *Where is he going?*

she stomps   *Why's he always late?*

Chill out, Rissa Marta says

His mom just went to work   He has to go back and check

on his brother   Whatever Clarissa responds   *He's still late*

Oh my god sighs Faith   *So what?*

                                    Okay I say

Listen   stop fighting   We're here because   my parents

are breaking up

                        What? everyone shouts at once

Like divorced? Faith asks   *Or is your dad just at your uncle*

Aaron's again?

                        Yes and yes I croak

then begin to sob   *Oh, snap!* says Marta   reaching

to give me a hug

                        You have got to stop saying that

Clarissa mutters under her breath

                                    Enough Faith says

motioning at Clarissa   to join in the hug   we're all tangled

in an embrace   when Dario rides up laughing   *It's like*

Woodstock up in here!

                        Marta leans over   whisper-fills-him-in

Oh, dip Dario looks up   *This is serious*

                                    Well, duh says Clarissa

But what's it all mean? she adds   *Like, are you moving?*

I rub my eyes with my sleeve   pry myself loose from the group

I am definitely not moving I declare   *I don't care if they want to*

I'm not leaving our block   *We've already moved enough*

That is one hundred percent true says Marta   *No denying it*

she shakes her head   *You've already moved like five times*

in your life

                    You can always come and live with me Faith says

a Blow Pop wedged between her teeth   *Don't be stupid* Clarissa

jumps in   *Alma has to live with her family*   *Plus the kids*

always stay with the mom

                    Faith rolls her eyes   turns

to Marta who adds   *Well, we're your family too*   *Word* Dario

agrees   *But you can't live with me*   *My mom would totally*

freak out   *Plus you would have to sleep*   *on the couch*

with my cousin

              Thanks, guys I smile through tears

I wish my parents would get divorced   Clarissa laments

Ay dios mío Marta mutters   *You can't say that*

Clarissa folds her arms across her chest   *I just did* she says

Well, I don't Marta frowns   *Plus, that's bad luck* Dario adds

Besides Faith interrupts   *parents are going to do what*

they want to do   There's no stopping them   turning

to me, Faith adds   *I mean, your mom and dad fight*

all the time, right?   And mine are always drunk

                                                            What?

Dario says   his voice snaps like a stick   we all freeze up

as he stares at Faith for a second   like she's just

What? It's true   Faith waves her hand like   *Get over it*

which we do

                              quickly shifting   we park ourselves

on Marta's stoop   Clarissa passes around the bag

of Blow Pops to change the mood   Dario hands me one

and adds   *Things are gonna be okay   It just feels messed up*

because it's new   I guess I reply   *I mean, thanks* I say

But I hate grape   Okay Dario smiles

                                        Same here

188

Underwater

parable :
a usually short fictitious story that illustrates
a moral attitude or a religious principle

My mother likes   to speak in parables sometimes   meaning

she'll tell me   a random story about life   then leave it to me

to figure out the point   which is irritating   especially if

I ask advice about a dilemma   or a question I have

like when I ask my mom
                                        Why San Francisco?

she says *I remember once*   then starts talking about

the time she was on Fire Island   and almost drowned

how she didn't know   the undertow was so strong   or

that she'd been in the water   for so long   how my dad

was on the blanket   reading a book
                                                    as a riptide

took my mom   way out beyond the dinghies   how

she swam hard and steady   toward the shore even though

the people and the seawall   weren't getting any closer

she just pressed on

                            until she made her way

back   where Dad   and other people had begun gathering

waving her in   calling out *Careful!*   about the rocks

that not realizing   it was a riptide   may have saved her life

because she didn't panic   I roll my eyes   *What does this*

have to do with San Francisco? I sigh

Kiddo

Kid, what changed your mood
you've gone all sad, so I feel sad too

—The Pretenders, "Kid"

Oh my god, please   Please, stop calling me "kiddo"

I am saying to my dad   who's drinking coffee

with an anguished expression on his face

Okay

he says smoothing his hair   reaching for my hand

I love you, kiddo   I mean, argh! Jeez!   That's a tough

habit to break   It's just that this is rough and I love you

I love you too, Dad   But no more "kiddo," okay?

How about "kid"? he brightens   *Less babyish, right?*

Okay, fine I sigh   *So, what's going to happen, Dad?*

I mean, what is happening?

Well

my dad clears his throat   *Your mom and I love you*

very much and we want you to know   it's not your fault

I know I say impatiently   *You don't have to do*

the whole divorce-talk thing   I've heard all about it

from Tara and Jennifer and Josh

                                            Tara's parents too?

Dad asks   *Yeah* I say   *And her dad's already split*

with his new wife   Dad hangs his head for a moment

in disbelief   *Good grief* he sighs   *It's like a disease*

Or bad luck I offer   Dad takes a gulp of coffee

Luck had nothing to do with this   shaking his head

he says   *We made our own choices   You understand?*

I don't want you going around thinking   if you hadn't

walked under that ladder   or if a black cat hadn't

crossed our path   this wouldn't have happened   We all

saw this coming   Can we agree on that?

                                            Yeah I nod

Okay he says   *It's late   Let's talk more in the morning*

reaching for the kitchen light   *Hey* my dad adds

We're all going to get through this   You're my kid, okay?

                                            Okay I say

Bright Side

You have to look on the bright side   Tara is saying

while banging her pen   on the metal handrail   so it

clangs like a gong
                        we should be in class

but we're standing on the stairs   same as every Tuesday

second period   when we all get bathroom passes

so we can catch up before lunch   since lunch is total

chaos and it's sometimes   hard to talk
                                        I mean

Tara explains   *You get a lot of stuff   from your grandparents*

and family and friends   You know, because everyone feels

so bad   Is that why you have two Walkmen? I ask

Exactly she says   giving the banister another whack

with her Bic
                Wait says Jennifer S.

Did you just say "two Walkmen"?   *Yeah* I answer *Why?*

Wouldn't it be . . . she starts   then stops to think *"Walkmanzzzz"*

with an s?
                What? The plural of "man" is "men" I explain

Hence, "Walkmen"

        Well, okay Jennifer S. concedes

But that sounds weird   Right?   she turns to Tara

who continues *You should get Atari   What?* I say

For Christmas?   No Jennifer S. laughs   *She means*

for the divorce

        For the divorce? I snort

Like I should make a list?

        Tara and Jennifer S. nod

their heads *Yes*   then watching my eyes go wide   begin shaking

their heads *No*   as in   *Okay-that-sounds-wrong-but-you-are-*

being-totally-impractical

        You're going to need   two of every-

thing anyway Jennifer S. says   *That's right* Tara agrees

Between the three apartments   I'm always losing everything

Three? Jennifer S. and I repeat in unison   *Greg* Tara rolls her eyes

Greg! Josh echoes from the landing above

        Jeez! Don't sneak up

on us!   Tara calls out   *Where've you been?* I ask

Richter wouldn't give me a pass   He wanted to know why I have

to go to the bathroom   every Tuesday at the same exact time

I told him "That's just how my bladder works" Josh laughs

Finally, he was like "Okay, enough about your bladder"

Yup Tara claps   *I just tell Mr. Tucci I am menstruating*

Wait Jennifer S. cuts in   *You don't actually say "menstruating"*

Sure, I do Tara replies   *Otherwise, he'd never let me go*

What? I ask   *He thinks you get your period every week?*

I have no idea Tara says   *But ever since I started saying*

"menstruating"   he just hands me the pass

No questions asked
                        I am definitely trying that I say

Same here Josh says   and we all laugh   *But really, Alma*

Tara adds   *You should totally ask for Atari*
                                    What?

Josh breaks in   *Are we talking guilty-parent gifts again?*

What? This is a thing?   I ask in disbelief

Welcome to the big leagues says Josh   *Best Christmas ever*

Oh no, Christmas I moan   smoothing my ponytail

as a lump rises in my throat
                        Yeah

says Jennifer S.   *The first one sucks but it gets better even if I do still cry a little every night*

Every night?

Really? Tara asks   *But your parents got divorced*

when you were five   So? shrugs Jennifer S.   *So, okay*

Tara smiles *That's all right   It's all fine* says Josh

As long as your dad   doesn't end up   permanently angry

like mine   Yeah says Jennifer S.

Permanent is a really long time

Heroes

A Hero Ain't Nothin' but a Sandwich   is a book about a boy

who becomes a junkie   meaning heroin addict

not homeless person   Jason from homeroom

with the Black Power pick   did a report on it

in sixth grade
                           Tara and I watched the film

after school last year   at the Museum of Broadcasting

it was sappy   tugged at your heartstrings so hard   I could

feel the story   trying to tell me what   to feel and think

if it had been real life   the boy would have ended up

dead on the street or in a doorway
                                            so when Ms. Foster

assigned an essay on heroes   I thought *sandwich*

suddenly felt cranky enough   to want to break my pencil

or bike around my block   a hundred times
                                                    like we're being

forced to believe an idea   that doesn't exist   that grown-

ups create like myths   for kids to write about   to fill

the time   when we should be screaming our heads off

outside   or listening to "Heroes" by David Bowie   which

is what I am doing right now   because it makes me feel

invincible   to listen on my Walkman in my room   as I write

my essay   about Bowie being a hero   because he acts

and dresses exactly how he feels   even if it means wearing

a dress   while pushing a baby carriage   through the fancy

streets of London   David Bowie will do it   brave and unique

to me he's   not just an artist   but an actual work of art

always changing   yet always the same   like he knows fame

is a myth   that he's playing with

                                        not letting it play him

Wisdom

Clarissa is snapping   a Chinese jump rope   hard

on the pavement like a whip   watching Miguel cruise

by on his bike   he's on the opposite side of the street

but Clarissa is making a point of it   staring hard at Miguel

with laser-like eyes   her jaw grinding a piece of purple

Bubble Yum

          C'mon, stop I say   *What?* asks Clarissa

You know I go   *Don't act obnoxious*   she turns to me

Have you guys even talked since the roof thing?   *Nope* I shake

my head   *Not for two weeks*   *I told my mom about me*

and Miguel   *about him punching Dario*   *calling him a faggot*

You know what she said?   *What?* Clarissa shrugs

she said *Honey, that's a red flag*   *Meaning what?* asks Clarissa

Red flag meaning bad sign   I explain   *about his personality*

Meaning he would make a bad boyfriend

                          So true

Clarissa nods   *Ancient Chinese wisdom*   she says bowing

her head   her hands together as if for prayer

That's from the detergent commercial! I shout

Oh my god, the only Chinese woman on TV   *and she*

works in a laundry!   *I know* Clarissa   laughs and claps

You wouldn't believe how much grief   I get at school

I bet I say   *And it's "ancient Chinese secret" not "wisdom"*

Oh yeah smiles Clarissa   *How about "Alma's mother's*

ancient Chinese secret wisdom"?

That too I laugh *That too*

Mystery: Logistics

We're sitting in the kitchen   and just as my mom predicted

I get quiet   when it's the three of us   my parents each

have their hands clasped   and resting on the dining table

like students at a desk   *This is weird* I say   *Why are you*

acting this way?
                    What way? my dad asks

Like we're at church or something I say   *Like someone's*

died   You're right my dad clears his throat   glancing quickly

at my mom   he smiles *Let's lighten this up   We're just here*

to discuss logistics   How things are going to work he adds

Okay I say   my voice lifting   as if it's a question

I am going to San Francisco   my mom begins   *for the summer*

to see Anne my old college friend   That will give me and Dad

some time and space to sort things through   I was thinking

you could join me for the month of August
                                            But I say

already feeling slightly panicked   *I start high school*

in September   I know, honey my mom responds

But it's beautiful out there   I want you to see it

smoothing my ponytail   I mumble-huff   *Whatever*

And says my dad upbeat   like he's won a raffle or something

I am going to stay at Uncle Aaron's   until Mom leaves

for San Francisco

                            Wait I say   *Where am I staying?*

Here! they both respond   *This is your home* my dad adds

Well, at least we agree on that   I snort   shaking my leg

under the table   *Okay* I say *Are we done?*   *Do you have*

any questions?   my mom asks   *Anything you want*

to talk about?   stroking my hand   *Not really* I answer

looking at the floor   *I'm just happy I don't have to move*

Also, I need five dollars to buy tampons

                                      Sure my mom says

reaching for her purse   on the counter   *Here's ten*

she says   *Maybe buy some snacks   for when you're*

hanging out with your friends?

                              Thanks I jam

the bill   into the back pocket of my cutoffs   and stand up

Are we done?   *Yes*   my mom and dad say together

their clasped hands back on the table   *Okay* I say   *I love you*

guys, but I hope you know   this meeting was totally pointless

Pointless

parable :
a usually short fictitious story that illustrates
a moral attitude or a religious principle

My mother likes   to speak in parables sometimes   meaning

she'll tell me   a random story about life

                          then leave it to me

to figure out the point   which is pointless   when it comes

to my grandparents   because I barely understand   where

they're coming from   half the time anyway   so when

my mom tells me   about the ill-fated cake   her friend

once made for Grandmother's banquet   I am mystified

by the circumstances and consequences alike

                          the cake

was white   wrong choice for a Chinese birthday

but her friend didn't know   was hurt that   no one thanked her

when she unveiled the dessert   which might as well have

been a pile of bones   shocking display of bad luck

that it was right   at the center of the table   beside

the faded porcelain pot and teacups

                                to make

matters worse   when my mother   cut the cake

and offered Grandmother   a slice on a plate   her friend

grabbed her wrist   swift as wind   whispered *Oh no!*

I think those dots are mold   my mother told her mother

in Chinese   that the icing had curdled in the heat   that

those spots weren't the currants   they appeared to be

but Grandmother and everyone else   just went on to eat

the entire thing   as if admitting   that the cream

had turned   would have turned her dessert   into a cake

of death   as if to speak of it   would have stolen her

last breath   as if so much bad luck   in a single day

didn't exist

                 if no one ever spoke of it

Speak of It

Clarissa is scarfing takeout   rice drizzled with soy sauce

I'm peering into a hand mirror   applying my new root-beer-

flavored lip gloss
                              we're sitting on her stoop

What is it with Chinese people? I say   *Or is it just my mom's*

family that behaves this way?   What way? Clarissa asks

Like how they don't know   your parents are splitting up?

Yeah I nod   tilting my face away from the sun   so I can get

a good look at my lips   *Plus* I add   *the only one who really*

talks about stuff is my dad
                              Well, okay says Clarissa

But Faith complains that   her parents never talk about

anything either   and they're not Chinese   I mean,

their ancestors came over on the Mayflower
                                        For real,

with the Pilgrims I laugh and blot my lips   on the back

of my hand   *I just don't understand   Not talking*

about things   doesn't make them go away
                                        Well, it's so

they don't seem real   You know, nobody wants to speak

things into being
                         I kiss the air   ask Clarissa

what she means   *Like how Chinese people are obsessed*

with bad luck she says   *Like if you say something bad*

you could make it happen
                                      I know, but I don't believe that

I say *That's not true*   I do Clarissa replies   *I told my mom*

she should divorce my dad   precisely because I want that

to happen!   You did? I laugh
                                      But Clarissa shakes

her head *she won't*   Chinese people never get divorced

What do you mean? I object   My mom's Chinese!

True nods Clarissa   *But she already broke the rules*

Maybe I shrug   I don't think you can choose

who you fall in love with   only maybe what you do

once you've fallen

Space Oddity

I'm stepping thro the door
And I'm floating in a most peculiar way
And the stars look very different today

> —David Bowie, "Space Oddity"

David Bowie is clever with words   like how his song

"Space Oddity" is a play on *Space Odyssey*   which is an old

movie about a bunch of guys   who go on a mission

to outer space   which you'd think   would be great

but which David Bowie   makes sound lonesome   with his sad

music slow as a lullaby

                I'm eating the freeze-dried astronaut

ice cream I bought at the gift shop   on our field trip

to the Museum of Natural History   thinking about this

and also about   how the trip wasn't just   to the gift shop

but how that's the part   everyone remembers   except for

the amazing dioramas   with the bison and the deer

and the Native Americans with spears   who Mr. Richter kept

calling *Indians*   even though we told him   *People don't say that anymore*   that he should know   since he's a social studies

teacher   which made Mr. Richter get defensive   yell for us

to *settle down*   which we mostly did   until this kid Nathaniel

got caught trying   to shoplift a pack of gum

while Mr. Richter

was apologizing to the manager   at the back of the store

some other kids   started stuffing lollipops   into their pockets

as the cashier watched silently   with pursed lips

a girl

named Samantha opened her jacket   gestured with her chin

at me to take one   so I grabbed a green apple   shoved it

into my pocket   for the ride back on the bus   Mr. Richter

wanted to know

Where did that come from?

It was in my lunch I huffed   pretending to be offended

Okay, Rosen! he barked   *But I'm putting the kibosh*

on shoplifting!   *Yeah, okay* I sighed   adding *Whatever "kibosh"*

means even though I knew   exactly what he meant I am

remembering this   thinking about time and space   and their

infinite range   when my brain starts   itching to make a list

before I know it my hand grabs a pen   and I'm writing:

Kinds of Space

outer   deep   personal   mental   physical

limited   emotional   creative   social

office   storage   shelf   parking   breathing

empty   space   where   Dad used to place

his head   next to Mom   as they slept   in their bed

counter   space   where   Dad's   cup

used to   be   now it's just   Mom   and me

space oddity   lonesome   kind of   lullaby   inside

Mental Kung Fu

mantra :
1 : (originally in Hinduism and Buddhism)
a word or sound repeated to aid concentration
in meditation
2 : a statement or slogan repeated frequently

I'm not moving

I'm not moving

I'm not moving

I'm not moving

I'm not moving

I'm not moving

I'm not moving

I'm not moving

I'm not moving

I'm not moving

Walk Home

I have cramps   my backpack weighs a ton   and the classrooms

were hot and the windows were stuck   and I stepped on

five cracks just walking   to the corner of Fourteenth Street

a ton of bad luck racked up   only steps from school   waiting

for the light   I feel a tap on my shoulder   turn to see Ms. Nola

her amber Afro backlit by the sun   glowing and shifting

with the breeze

                  Alma she says   a little out of breath

Oh, hey I say   *Alma, honey, I wanted to catch you   You missed*

your check-in with me this week

                        I had cramps I shrug

the streetlight turns to WALK   so we do   heading south

down Eighth Avenue   Ms. Nola keeps pace with me

I'm walking quickly   like I tend to   as if I am trying

to lose her   which I am not   but I'm not used to

hanging out with teachers   so to make conversation I go

This is like that poster   Which one? Ms. Nola asks   putting on

a pair of giant tortoise sunglasses

                    The one in your office

that says   "We're all just walking each other home"

she nods from behind her purple lenses   *Oh, Ram Dass*

He's a spiritual leader   It's about helping each other

through life

                    Interesting I say   *So, are you walking*

me home? I joke   *How about halfway?* Ms. Nola proposes

School's ending in a couple of weeks   I just want to see how

you are   I know your parents are getting divorced

Wait I stop   *Who told you that? Tara?*   No Ms. Nola

explains   *Your parents called me   Well, separately*

But they each gave me a call

                         Oh my god I start walking again

this time superfast   *Listen* Ms. Nola says   *They just thought*

I should know   It's an important life change   so I was

disappointed   when you didn't come to check-in   she puts

her hand on my shoulder

                         I told you I say   looking away

I had cramps   And it's not like it was a surprise   They used

to fight all the time

                    I hear you Ms. Nola says

But it still might make you sad   and maybe angry too?

we halt at the corner   crowd up with a cluster of people

on Sixth Avenue   watching a fleet of police cars streak

through hot traffic   lights flashing sirens blaring

once the signal changes   and the noise has faded

we begin walking again   this time in silence

as we're about to reach Fifth   Ms. Nola pauses and says

Take this   handing me a slip of paper   *We only have*

one more check-in   before school ends and then it's all

meetings for me   I hope to see you   so you don't get marked

"cutting"   But if I don't   here's my phone number

You can call me if you want   Anytime
                                              Thanks I look

at the paper   *I heard you live in Brooklyn, right?*

Yes says Ms. Nola
                    My grandma Miriam lived in Brooklyn

I remember you telling me that she nods   *Your first name*

is Lovelie? I half laugh   *Yup* Ms. Nola smiles   *That's cool* I say

I always thought so she agrees   adding briskly *All right, Alma*

You go home now and I'll take my train   Try not to skip

check-in again, Miss Cramps
                              Okay I say folding the paper

                    I'll try

List of Things I Won't

do tonight's science homework

do drugs

do heroin

get married

get divorced

get a boyfriend

keep a boyfriend who punches people and calls them faggot

keep a book open all night so that its spine cracks

keep letting my dad call me "kiddo"

forget my friends

forget my grandma Miriam

forget who loves me and who I love back

Red Flags

Faith is French-braiding my hair   up on her roof   telling me

I should give Miguel   a chance to explain

Explain what?

I say   *I just don't want to hang out with him anymore*

Right says Faith   *But maybe if he could tell you*   *why he got*

so mad—   *You don't understand!* I cut her off   *It's not why*

he got mad   *It's what he did when he got mad*   *It's a red flag*

Red means stop   *Don't you know that?*

I'm not stupid

Faith says   parting my hair   *I know red means stop*

It's just unfair   *not to give him a second chance*

I never said you were stupid   I answer glancing

back at her

Don't move   Faith steadies my head

with the comb   *Jeez* she mumbles   raking a stubborn knot

You have so much hair   *You're lucky, Alma*   *It's not fine*

like mine   *Lucky?* I laugh   *If I were lucky, Miguel*

wouldn't have ended up being such a jerk

And my parents wouldn't be getting divorced

Wait

says Faith   *Those things have nothing to do with luck*

They're messed up   but it's not about luck   Besides, I'm

not very lucky either   I mean, my parents are alcoholics

Wow I say   *Is that the actual word you'd use?*

Well, yeah sighs Faith   *It's pretty obvious, isn't it?*

They're like one gigantic red flag she snorts   twisting

the elastic   around the tail of my hair   *Et voilà!* she says

dropping the braid against my back   where it plunks

                                        with a gentle thud

Stairwell

I don't mean to brag, I don't mean to boast
But we like hot butter on our breakfast toast

—The Sugarhill Gang, "Rapper's Delight"

Well, it happened on the stairs   I am telling Tara and Jennifer S.

So fast I wasn't prepared
                              Oh my god says Tara

Oh my god says Jennifer S.   *We were just laughing*

singing Sugarhill Gang   like we sometimes do   trying to see

who could get to the end   when bam!   all of a sudden

he's on me   and I just kept thinking   the bell is going to ring

and people will see him   trying to kiss me   But truthfully,

I was so surprised   I froze
                              No says Tara

No says Jennifer S.   *Yes I say   I mean, I thought Josh was gay*

You didn't say that, did you? Tara gasps   *Yes* I nod

No says Jennifer S.   No chimes Tara   *I did* I insist

Oh my god they both hiss   *But then I said "That's okay"*

So, we kissed a little anyway   Tara is shaking her head

waving her arms   going *I just cannot*   Jennifer S. finishes

her sentence   *believe this*

                              Well I say

You better believe it   And you better not say a word

If Josh heard that I told you   he would be upset

So asks Tara *does he think he's gay?   Tough to say* I sigh

I think he is trying to figure it out   Maybe that's what

this was about

                              Probably adds Tara

Perhaps shrugs Jennifer S.   *Either way* I say

Awkward!   they both shout

Awkward

Check-in with Ms. Nola   isn't awkward exactly   but it feels

different than it usually does   maybe it's because soon

I'll be leaving this school forever   maybe it's because

I feel different about Ms. Nola   ever since she walked me

halfway home   she seems more familiar to me   than she

did before

here in her office   cradling the phone

between her shoulder and her ear   flicking lint off

her blouse   *Come in* she mouths   motioning to the chair

where I sit and pretend not to listen   as she discusses

some kind of *rubric for the district*   *blah blah blah*

accountability   Ms. Nola smiles and rolls her eyes

like *Can you believe I have to deal with this?*   looking like

she actually can't believe she does   when she finally

hangs up   there's a light glint of sweat   above her lip

and another streak glistening   along her hairline

This office   I think to myself   *is hotter than Hades*

So, what's going on? Ms. Nola smiles

I'm fine I say   *I mean, nothing much*   *You know* I add *same old*

Well Ms. Nola   clasps her hands and leans in   *Then tell me*

something new

the first thing that comes to mind

is Josh kissing me on the stairs   but I'm scared

to mention that   because what if she wants to talk

about him being gay   I wouldn't know what to say

that's a very personal question   really none of her

business   maybe even none of mine

my mind races

to find a topic   we haven't covered   *I got my period* I offer

I figured Ms. Nola nods   *Since you missed our last check-in*

due to cramps   she smiles, making quotation marks

in the air around the *cramps* part

Yes I say

they can get really bad   *Indeed* Ms. Nola agrees   shifting

in her swivel chair   *So, how's it going at home?* she wants

to know

All right I start   *My dad is staying at my uncle's*

until my mom goes to California   *for the summer*

And how does that feel? Ms. Nola asks

Well, he used

220

to do that sometimes   but this time feels weird

because you know   he's not coming back   I mean,

he is   but not with my mom   so that's new

And how about you? says Ms. Nola   crossing her legs

I'm just happy   I don't have to move I begin   Like,

I knew this kid   who had a friend who   when his parents

got divorced   ended up staying in their apartment

with his sister   and it was his mom and dad

who switched off   coming to stay   That way the kids

weren't the ones   who had to lug their duffels on the train

every other Friday   like Tara who practically breaks her back

carrying her weekend bag   even if she does tend to overpack

Interesting muses Ms. Nola   Is that something   you'd want

your parents to consider?
                                        Well, there's only one of me I say

We'd need three apartments   which would cost a lot

Unless my mom lived with her parents   and my dad lived

with Uncle Aaron   but that would never happen   because

my grandparents   don't even know about the divorce

And why is that? asks Ms. Nola
                                        Nobody wants

to give them sad news I explain   *It gets them really*

worked up   about bad luck and shame   That's why

I didn't meet them   until I was eight   I mean,

they didn't even know about me   until after I was born

So, you can see   it's pretty messed up

If you could tell

your grandparents about what's happening   what would

you say?   Ms. Nola wants to know

pausing to smooth

my ponytail   I notice the dusty macramé plant holder

is no longer holding a plant   *I guess* I start by clearing

my throat   *I'd say   things come and go*

And we must let them?   Is that a question? asks Ms. Nola

No I answer   *It's mental kung fu*

Bad Form

Bad form   sometimes means flipping a fish   or crossing

your chopsticks   but right now   it means high school

registration   which gives me *agita*   which is a word

Grandma Miriam would use   when she felt stressed

like when she'd say to my dad   *For crying out loud,*

stop driving that cab   You're giving us all agita!

which must be a synonym   for *administrative paperwork*

because they share symptoms

like heart-racing

perspiration and feeling flustered   in the office

when faced with all these forms

plus Mr. Gordon

peering over your shoulder   acting like you might

spell your own name wrong   if he wasn't there

to make sure   which is also bad form

because hasn't he heard   of personal space

I mean, jeez

Dream of the Persephones

In the dream of the Persephones   all the Girls on our block

are named for the Greek goddess   of harvest and fertility

Persephone   whose own father allowed her to be

kidnapped by Hades   just because Hades was in love

with her   Why Zeus would do that   is a mystery to me

since he should have wanted to keep her safe   should

have let her mother, Demeter   help decide Persephone's

fate or better yet   have let Persephone choose her

own path
                    but back to the Girls

in my dream   stalking doorways   wearing snakes for hair

like Medusa   and holding branches of wheat   as symbols

of their fecundity   meaning they can get pregnant   so that

the men know to be careful   even if men like that are not

likely to care about   carefulness or consequences

but back to the Girls
                                and the scarlet pomegranates

which they carry in bags   which break open like eggs

when hurled by the Girls   at the men pulling up in sedans

and which leave seeds   scattered like bloody teeth

across the sidewalk
                         in the myth   not my dream

Persephone is tricked by Hades   into eating a single

ruby kernel before leaving   to see her mother

not knowing that   if she eats in the underworld

she'll be forced to always return   unlike the Girls

on my block   who can never leave   this street

                              they call home

Survival

When my dad asks me   if I've had any dreams lately

we are sharing a toasted bagel   with cream cheese and chives

my favorite kind   at our favorite place on Second Avenue

No I mumble   through a mouthful of schmear

                                        Here

he laughs   handing me a napkin   even though the dream

of the Persephones is still fresh   in my mind   I don't want to

spend the time we have   before my dad goes back

to Uncle Aaron's   analyzing my dream   I think I know what

it means   I don't always need my dad   to explain things

for me

            this one was not

about boys   more about men   plus when Faith asked me

the other day   what I thought it meant   I said *Survival*

and she nodded her head

                        like that made perfect sense

Hands-On Experiment

I hate the way   *Tucci keeps repeating "hands-on"*

Jennifer S. is complaining   trying to scratch her name

with a bent paper clip   into the surface of the steel lab counter

He's just explaining   *that we get to put our hands on*

everything   Josh smirks   *Don't be a jerk* Tara says

How is that being a jerk? Josh asks   holding his arms up

like *I surrender*

                    You don't care

because you're a guy Jennifer S. adds   Tara nods and says

Don't you hear his tone?   *Plus, the way he keeps looking*

at Angela's chest   *So gross!*

                                        I turn to Josh

and say *You're practically*   *the only guy who doesn't*

Doesn't what? he asks

                    Stare at Angela's chest! we all hiss

Mr. Tucci interrupts   his never-ending speech   looks

at our table   asks *Is there an issue?*

                                    There are many issues

Tara whisper-laughs   under her breath   *What's that?*

Mr. Tucci puts down his chalk   walks over with a forced

sense of purpose   *Oh my god* Josh groans   *We're fine* I say

Sorry, Mr. Tucci   You were explaining   we have three choices,

right?

          Right he agrees

deciding to let it go   *For your final project   you can either*

guide a plant through a maze   which would involve

phototropism   make a rainbow of flames   which involves

various chemical reactions   or you can extract your own

DNA from cells in your cheek   Today you'll choose at your

group table   We'll start individual work next week

Here, take this Josh nudges Jennifer S.   passes her

his compass   in exchange for her twisted paper clip

Thanks she whispers   goes to work on deepening the *J*

she's engraved into the table   *I'm totally doing rainbow flames*

Josh says

          Not me Tara declares

You know, last year Melissa O'Hare   got second-degree burns

on her arm, right?   I'm doing the maze she adds

Plants are safe

          Me too Jennifer S. agrees   *How about you, Alma?*

I think I'll do DNA   *Isolate the strand* I say   Josh shakes

his head   *I'd only do that   if it could really tell me*

something

                                  Like what? Tara asks   *If you're gay?*

Tara! Jennifer S. says   clutching her forehead   Josh turns

toward me   I can see he's wondering   what I'd told them

Sure he says   *Or like if I'm really Polish*

                                              It's fine

if you're gay Jennifer S. says   *But it would suck to be Polish*

Tara adds

                            Why? I ask   *Because* Tara explains

people are always telling   stupid Polish jokes

about swimming halfway   across a river and back

Yeah I nod *But people can be really cruel   when it*

comes to being gay

                                    That's so true Jennifer S. says

Oh my god Tara grabs Josh's arm   *What if you're Polish*

and gay?   Josh shrugs *I guess I'm screwed if that's the case*

Don't worry Tara adds   *We love you anyway*

                                              Unhand me,

you wench Josh laughs   brandishing his bent-up paper clip

And stop staring at Angela's chest!

Futile Attempts

I write letters to Maureen   that I never send

because there's nowhere   to send them

these futile attempts   make me feel

sad and empty   but also like Maureen

can hear me   like she's listening

from another dimension

June 12, 1982

Dear Maureen,

Where are you? Are you happy? Are you safe?

I hope everything is okay wherever you are. It's superhot here and school's not even out. We all can't wait for them to open the pool, but it will be different without you. Maybe you'll be swimming in that lake, which sounds really great. Maybe you aren't near any water at all. Maybe you've moved to the desert. Speaking of bleak, Miguel and I aren't hanging out anymore. There was some drama, but it's not worth getting into. Let's just say: Red Flags.

Also, I filled out my registration for that arts high school uptown. I don't know which area will be my focus, but if I can do more art and just read, I will be happy. I haven't been drawing for a while, but this summer I'll probably get back into it.

Clarissa and Marta and Faith are busy doing their thing.
They wonder where you've gone, but not as much as me.
I remember your glasses and your blond eyelashes.

Please write back.
Love,
Alma

P.S. My parents are getting divorced.

P.P.S. But I don't have to move.

Now and Later

It's hot and I am sitting   in the shade of the tree

by my stoop   eating a freeze pop and reading

The Book of Lists   just because
                                when I spot Churro

waddling   down the other side of the street   being pulled

on his leash   by none other than Miguel   the poor dog

is salivating hard in the heat   his body slung so low

to the ground   I can imagine the pavement

scorching his fur
                    Miguel glances up

I quick turn back to my book   cheeks tingling

my hand tipping purple juice   onto the list

of *24 Noted People Who Never Married*   within

a few seconds   Miguel is crossing over   with Churro

tugging to give me a wet hello   *Hola, Churro* I say

petting his head as he licks   freeze pop dregs from the step

slobbers on my flip-flops   *Hey, what's up?* says Miguel

Not much I reply   *I was just getting ready to go inside*

and sit in front of the fan   *It's so hot for June*

Yeah Miguel nods   *We just got an air conditioner*

for our living room   if you want to come up

I close the book on my lap   shake my head   *That's okay*

I have some things to do today   You know, paperwork

for high school and stuff

                              Are you going to that arts school

you talked about way back? Miguel asks   *Wow* I nod

I can't believe you remember that   But yeah, I am

Miguel squats down   to scratch Churro behind the ears

I bet he says   *if they had a school   for people who like to think*

where they train you   to be a philosopher or something

you would probably go   Miguel half smiles   like it's still

our private joke   *But* he continues   *art school is cool*

I hope I shrug   *I only know a couple of people*

going there so . . .

                    Well, you're really creative Miguel says

You'll make friends   I guess I nod   *How about you?*

What are you doing?

                    Me? he says

I'm working at my uncle's garage this summer   Then going

to school with the crew   Nothing special standing up

Miguel adds   *Hey, I heard your parents are getting divorced*

my face suddenly feels hot   I can sense a light sweat

break out beneath my tank top   I reach to smooth

my ponytail   then stop and breathe   *That's true* I reply

in a mellow way   I don't really recognize

                                          closing his eyes

for a second Miguel says *I'm sorry*   *It's okay* I say

At least I don't have to move away   *That's good news* he agrees

I mean, that would suck   *I mean, for our block*

Yeah, anyway I say   scooping up my book   *I have to go now*

All right Miguel pats Churro   *Check you later, Alma*

Letter to Persephone

June 17, 1982

Dear Persephone,

 I should like science more than I do, but instead of listening to Mr. Tucci, I am writing to you. I sometimes write to my grandma Miriam when I want to talk. But as time goes on, I realize that writing to someone who doesn't write you back or to someone who is dead is sort of like talking in your head. I guess writing to a character in a myth isn't any different, but I think you would relate to parts of my life—if you were a real person, like me, who feels caught between places and the spaces in between. Or maybe I relate to you—even if my dad would never allow someone to kidnap me, even if I've never eaten a pomegranate.

 I've been thinking that your dad should have been looking out for you. No offense, but he should have struck down Hades with a lightning bolt, even if Hades is his brother. And your mother, Demeter, shouldn't have made the world go hungry just because she missed you, because that's a lot of suffering to spread around. But I get it. Hades, on the other hand, was manipulative when he tricked you into eating those seeds so that you would always have to return to the underworld. I don't think I would have fallen for that, but being stolen from your family sounds stressful. People make bad decisions when they are under pressure, so I completely understand. You were probably flustered and missing your mom.

Life can be difficult for mortals too. I find it helpful to have mantras like Ram Dass does. He's a spiritual teacher my guidance counselor told me about—which makes Ms. Nola sound like she'd be in a cult, but believe me, she is not! Mantras are kind of like tools for mental kung fu, which is something I use to help me get through my day. Phrases you can say to keep you calm.

Like right now, how Mr. Tucci is looking over to see if I am writing up my lab. He probably doubts it, since I am writing really fast. I usually take my time when it comes to science. Meanwhile, I am wondering how he can still be wearing that sweater in June—the same one, I should say, he's been sporting since Christmas, which someone in his family must have given him to replace the green one he had been wearing every day since September. Today, Mr. Tucci is totally perspiring. And it's gross. You wouldn't know about this, though, since you're probably always dressed in a toga. Ha ha ha . . .

If Mr. Tucci asks to see my paper, I will tell him I am menstruating, which will maybe make him go away.

Menstruation

Menstruation

Menstruation

can be a mantra too. But not one that would have saved you from Hades the god or Hades the place, since I am pretty sure goddesses don't menstruate. I am chanting "menstruation" in my head—

pretending to look at my notes, so that Mr. Tucci won't stop at my desk as he wanders around the class. We were supposed to have a test today, but either the new Xerox machine was on the blink or Mr. Tucci totally forgot. We aren't sure what to think, because Ms. Foster made copies just last period, and when we mentioned the exam, Mr. T. looked like he had no idea what we were talking about for a second. Then he cleared his throat, mumbled something about the copier, and started writing on the board.

In any case, everyone was relieved—especially me, since I had a hard time studying last night. All the terms, like "surfactant" and "surface tension," "active agent" and "catalyst," felt superabstract, kept slipping away, making me think instead about other, different kinds of change. Like how "surface tension" sounds like something you can feel when you walk into a room—especially if it's a kitchen where your parents are sitting after having talked all night, where they're staring into mugs of coffee like they're contemplating cups of poison. Shouting "Wake up!" would be one way to break the tension, a "surfactant" made of words. Or you could just grab your lunch and go to school, which is what I usually do. As Ms. Scappino, our gym teacher, says when we ask why she isn't yelling at the other kids for goofing off during volleyball: "You gotta pick your battles."

Or you could be an "active agent," something "that produces a reaction." Which is sometimes how I want to be—to not hold back from something I want to do or say. Like how I was the other day in social studies when Mr. Richter asked if we supported the death penalty. I raised my hand and said no. When he asked why, I told him that it's like "an eye for an eye"—which is in the Bible—and that I believe aliens exist more than I believe in God. The whole class was quiet for a second, until this kid Antonio goes, "You are SO going to hell." To which I said, "Better than the electric chair!" Everyone yelled "Oooooh" the way we do when there's going to be a fight. Mr. Richter was like, "Okay, let's stop there. Copy down the homework, everyone."

Or you could be a "catalyst," which is "a substance that increases the rate of a chemical reaction without undergoing any permanent chemical change." Which is also the opposite of how I am sometimes—when I feel paralyzed, unable to make anything happen faster than it would have without me. Or even at all.

All this got me thinking about fate, and about the three old women called the Fates that we talked about in Ms. Foster's class. Like Penelope, who makes a burial shroud for Laertes, the Fates also weave—only they create human destiny, meaning they hand out your fate. One Fate spins the cotton into thread, one Fate measures each person's allotment of thread, and one Fate cuts the thread—she's the one who decides when you're dead. Leading me to questions like:

1. When people—like my grandma Miriam—die of cancer, is that fate?
2. What if someone dies in a car crash? Is that just an accident?
3. When someone gets struck by lightning, is that nature? Or fate?
4. When people meet and fall in love, is that fate or just a question of who they choose to date?

5. When people fall out of love, is that because of fate or because of an "active agent"?
6. Can an "active agent" control her fate?
7. Are "catalysts" ever afraid?

The bell just rang!
Love,
Alma

Pop Rocks

Tara and Jennifer S. and I   are giggling and sizzling

cherry Pop Rocks   on our tongues   down the block

from school   we're lined up for a fire drill   when Josh

comes strolling up   *You guys ready for graduation?*

he wants to know

                          Yup we nod   *I already have my outfit*

I say *Sandals and a sundress*   *because you know that*

cafetorium is going to be   *hotter than Hades*

                                  Did you just say

"hotter than Hades"? Jennifer S. snickers   *You're such a nerd*

sometimes   *Whatever* I smile   flick a Pop Rock into her hair

Tara turns to Josh *You wearing a suit?*   *Nope, I'm actually going*

as David Bowie   *Wait, what?* Jennifer S. shrieks   *No way!*

the three of us scream   *Yep* Josh smiles   kicking the sidewalk

with his sneaker   *Ziggy Stardust with makeup and everything*

And your mom is good with this? Jennifer S. asks   *She's doing*

my face and hair Josh laughs   *Your mom is so cool* sighs Tara

So cool we all agree   *Originally* Josh says *I wanted to dress up*

as Blondie   *but my mom said people at school   aren't ready*

for that   Deborah Harry being a woman and all   Yeah I say

Too radical

                        Too bad, though Tara mumbles

through a mouthful of Pop Rocks   *She's so beautiful*

You know I say   *I once saw Debbie Harry at this Ukrainian*

restaurant near my house   No way Josh says *You're so lucky*

Nothing ever happens where we live

                                        Plus I add

she looked exactly like she did   when she hosted

Saturday Night Live *last year   Only no tuxedo*

Oh my god Tara cuts in   *Josh! You could wear lipstick*

and a tux!   Josh shakes his head   *There's no way*

I'm wearing a tux   No way

Creation Myth

June 20, 1982
Alma Rosen
English 8/Foster HR 302

WRITTEN BY HERSELF

I was born in minutes in my mother's kitchen,

in a wok tossed with ginger and scallions,

and matzoh brei on the side.

My mother heard my name whispered

in the sizzling oil of her wok.

"Alma," it said. "Alma," she said.

My father heard my mother say my name

in her sleep. He thought it was a dream—

her soul awake and speaking in the middle

of the night, the sound of flight.

So, he said "Alma" too.

And I took form—the form of a girl

who was a phoenix in her previous life,

a bird who had risen from the ashes of a city

burned down to the ground, a bird who soared

through rain and clouds toward her home

in the hot, hot sun.

I was born to be superstitious, but I am not.

I lived on a dangerous block, but I was not afraid.

I made my way on a bike that had wings.

I wore a crown made of music that could sing.

I was free as I wanted to be.

To make choices and mistakes.

To stay out of harm's way.

To be at home wherever I go.

Ms. Foster gave me a 92   wrote *I like what you wrote here,*

Alma   It's not quite the essay I assigned   More like pictures

from your mind   More like a poem, perhaps? Can I share this

with the class?   I said she could

Sometimes You Feel Like a Nut

Sometimes you feel like a nut. Sometimes you don't.
Almond Joy's got nuts. Mounds don't.

—TV commercial, 1977

I am spinning the lazy Susan   at the center of the banquet

table   loaded with wobbling bottles of soy sauce

Coca-Cola and Johnnie Walker Black   the last one being

a fifth of scotch   no one ever opens   because it's only

there to show it's a fancy occasion   like a graduation

which it is   even if it's only from eighth grade

it's still

a big deal or else   why would my grandparents have come

all the way from Chinatown   to sit in the humid cafetorium

at my school surrounded by wilting balloons   only to go back

home again   so they could get Great-grandmother   and bring

her by cab to the restaurant

so she could give me this special pen

a black-and-gold Mark Cross   in a velvet box

which chokes me up　　because Great-grandmother's hands

are so fragile　　her jade bangle heavy as a weight　　around her

thin wrist as she steadies herself　　to squeeze my hand and smile

to let me know she's proud　　I am spinning the lazy Susan

at the center of the banquet table　　irritated by the stilted

conversation　　when without even thinking　　I blurt out

So, Mom and Dad are getting divorced　　but that's okay

because I don't have to move
　　　　　　　　　　　　　　　the silence is so swift

and complete　　it feels like a smack on the cheek　　like

a complete failure of mental kung fu　　which I can tell

it is　　from the way my mom is gripping her chopsticks

the way my dad is smoothing his hair　　my grandmother

turns to her daughter　　begins speaking Chinese

very quickly　　more quickly than I have　　ever heard

her speak　　she is not shouting　　sounds more like she

is scolding a child and it hurts
　　　　　　　　　　　　　　　the only word I can

make out is *lofan*　　which is what they call my dad

not as an insult so much   as because history   which

feels unfair   but it's hard to care   when Grandmother

breaks off from her speech   all the grandparents

are staring at me   then staring at my parents   then

back at me
                    to disrupt the hush

I clear my throat   say very loudly   *Well, it's true*

which does not improve the situation   which actually causes

my mother to grab her purse and hiss   *This dinner is through*

which it mostly is   but which is beside the point   because

what a mess
                    it's twilight

my mom my dad and me   are walking north in silence

along the Bowery   past the old hotels and restaurant supply

shops with their rows of steel pots and pans   glowing blue

in the light of the hour   *Okay* my dad says   at the corner

of Houston   *This is me*   meaning he's going to take

the subway back   to Uncle Aaron's on the Upper East Side

Okay I say *Bye*   then burst out crying   *I'm sorry* I sob

It's okay says my mom   *It's okay* my dad says   *They had*

to find out sooner or later   my mother strokes my hair

which calms me down   for the moment
                                                                      but the next day

when I tell Marta what happened   she says
                                                                      Ay dios mío,

Alma, what are you, nuts?   and I am crying all over again

Nuts

When I was little   my dad used to call me   *the cashew of his eye*

instead of the *apple*   because apples aren't that special

but cashews are delectable   and he loves them almost

as much as me and coffee   especially the fancy roasted kind

Grandma Miriam used to keep   in a cut-crystal dish

in her living room   for when people came to visit   people

like me and my dad   who would gobble them up   as soon

as we sat down   on her green floral couch   me secretly

using the doily on its armrest   to dust the excess salt

from my fingertips   my dad secretly winking at me

as Grandma Miriam would breeze in   from the kitchen

carrying cans of cream soda   smiling *Well, someone*

couldn't resist!
                    I am sitting on my steps

remembering this   when Dario rolls up on a new bike

that's not as tiny as his old one   *Nice bike* I say   pulling

my headphones   down around my neck
                                            Thanks

Dario says *It used to be my cousin's*   *Cool* I say tearing open the orange wrapper of my Reggie Bar   I break off a piece

and hold it out   *Want some?*

                                     Sure he says

taking the chunk   of quickly melting chocolate   *Thanks*

he shoves it into his mouth   garbles *You know Reggie*

Jackson's a jerk, right?   *No, what do you mean?*   Well Dario

begins *my uncle knows this guy from work who was once*

in an elevator uptown   when Reggie Jackson gets in   and this

little kid asks him for his autograph   You know what he says?

No, what?

                         He told the kid to get lost!

What? I wave my hand   *That can't be true* I say

Who would say that to a kid?   I mean,

he's a Yankee

                  I know Dario nods *Nuts, right?*

Some kind of hero he says   shaking his head   *No class*

Well, he's no Jackie Robinson I laugh

                                But you have to admit

Dario adds   *his candy bar is pretty delicious   Not half*

as good as Twix I say   *Half is better than none* he answers

Good enough for some I say   *But we should probably*

                    switch to Baby Ruth

Nickels and Dimes

It's too hot for knishes   Clarissa is whining   as we glide down

First Avenue toward East Houston   school is out

but the pool doesn't open until noon   so we're tooling

around killing time   Dario has a paper bag   filled

with dimes   chiming in one hand   as he steers his bike

toward Yonah Schimmel's

I don't get why

you don't have any quarters or nickels or bills   Clarissa calls

over her shoulder   *Because* Dario yells back   *my mom always*

gives me the dimes from her purse   It's just this thing she's done

since I was five   Back when it was a big deal to get a dime

Oye! Marta shouts ahead   *Pay for me? Dario?   No tengo*

dinero hoy   All right, but you still owe me a slushie

I know, I know Marta says   *I'm gonna get a job, I swear*

we skid to a stop on the corner   where First and Houston meet

pile our bikes up on the street   then pile inside to buy

our knishes   double-wrapped in wax paper and foil

steaming in the heat   we sit along a ledge   on the shady side of the street and eat in silence

Oh, snap Marta says Look!

pointing down at a patch of pavement   between her feet

to a small plastic bag of marijuana   A nickel bag!

Clarissa hisses   reaching for it   Ew Marta says slapping

Clarissa's hand from the bag   Don't touch it! That's nasty!

What? whisper-shouts Clarissa   It's just weed

You don't know I break in   It could be laced with PCP

Clarissa rolls her eyes   I'm not going to smoke it   I just want

to see if it's real   she pinches open the tiny pouch   sniffs

its contents   Maybe we can sell it Dario suggests

What? Like dealers? I say No way!   Clarissa rubs her nose

It's real all right   Real strong too

Argh I moan

hopping off the ledge   I say Let's go home   Wait Dario says

Aren't we going to the pool?

Let's just go I insist

shaking my leg   looking both ways   Fine Clarissa snaps

slipping the pouch into her pocket   What are you doing? I ask

pointing to Clarissa's cutoffs   Throw it away! I say

Why are you so afraid of everything? Clarissa wants to know

It's not fear! I shout   *It's called intelligence   You want*

your parents to find it?   Your shorts probably already smell

I mean, what the hell, Clarissa?   Alma's right Dario sighs

gesturing with his bag of dimes   *We should just go*

Somebody probably dropped it   and I don't need to get

my ass kicked today, okay?   Clarissa flicks the packet

to the curb   *Okay* she calls   as she crosses

to get her bike
                        Happy?

Happy

Happiness is the public pool at noon   two hundred kids

splashing and peeing and screaming   not caring that

it's ninety degrees outside   as their bodies   waist-deep

in freezing   superchlorinated water   adjust

to the rhythm of summer   which is one long wave

of hanging out   endless candy and ice cream trucks

with almost no adults   and definitely no homework

the noise at the pool is a roar   and the air smells

like bleach   but each of us   would take this   over

the beach any day

She looks happy

Dario is saying to Marta   *Sí, se ve feliz* Marta agrees

glancing my way   *You talking about me?*   I paddle a little

closer   *What?* No says Dario   *Were so* I say   *My ears*

are burning   *What's that supposed to mean?* asks Marta

It's just an expression   *my grandma Miriam used to use*

It means you were talking about me   *Anyway* I turn to Dario

What? You think I look happy?   *Yeah* he shrugs *Happier*

I mean, than you have   *Why?* I ask   *Have I looked sad?*

Well, not sad Dario says   *Kind of far away, maybe*

You know, maybe thinking   about your parents and stuff?

I take this in for a minute   nod *Yeah   It's weird how it feels*

like there's a lot going on   but also nothing at all

Sort of like summer Dario offers   *Yes* I smile

                        A lot like summer

Free

I don't know why   I feel so free sometimes   speeding down

the street on my banana seat   the white tassels on my

handlebars splayed   like feathers in the wind   this doesn't

happen most days   but when it does   I could cruise around

my neighborhood for hours   my places and my people

just a blur   as I circle Tompkins Square   or St. Mark's Church

my ponytail whipping behind me   free to be me

going anywhere   I want to be

Okay

I'm back from having pizza   with Tara and Jennifer S.

before they leave for summer camp   my mom is sitting

on her bed   reading in front of the fan   wisps of her long hair

grazing the page of her open book

Whatcha reading? I say

sliding off my flip-flops   climbing up to curl   catlike

beside her   press my face   against the cool cotton sheet

The Color Purple *by Alice Walker* she replies   stroking my cheek

I tilt my head to see the cover   *What's it about?*

Well my mom begins   *it's a novel made of letters about*

a woman who—

An epistolary novel! I proclaim

poking the air with my finger   *Cool!*   *Yes* my mom smiles and

shakes her head   *I'm not even sure   if that's a word I knew*

before you came along

It means a story   told through letters

I explain   *Yes* my mom continues   *and the main character*

Celie writes letters to God   because she is suffering a lot

I just started but I can see   she needs someone to listen

Sometimes I used to write Grandma Miriam I say

That's wonderful my mom smiles   *Sometimes on paper*

or just in my mind

                Just in your mind is fine she replies

You're still creating that energy   putting it out there

I'm sure her spirit felt it   Yes I nod *Energy*

I sometimes think I feel her spirit   but I'm not sure if

it's me remembering her   like the energy of her memory

or what

        Well my mom says   *maybe it doesn't matter*

which just as long as she's with you   we sit in silence

for a moment   then my mom switches tone

So she begins   *I really want you to come*

to San Francisco with me for August

                        Argh I sit up

I don't want to miss the last month   before high school

starts   I feel like everything is going to change   I need

to be here

        Well my mom says taking my hand

things do change   not everything goes as planned

sometimes life gets in the way

Or San Francisco I say

Or San Francisco my mom repeats   *How about two weeks, then?*

First half of August?   *That way you can finish off the summer*

with your friends?   *I'll think about it* I sigh   *Okay?*

Okay my mom nods   and closes her book

Okay

Faith is in Nah-fuck-it   and Alisha who we never see

has a job at Twin Donut   so it's me and Clarissa and Marta

and Dario most of the time   at the pool   on a roof

or someone's stoop   which is fine   we're tight and get

along well
                    except when Miguel is out   hanging around

after his shift   at the garage   he always looks upset

his presence makes us tense   like he's trying not to seem

left out   by appearing to be busy   doing nothing   except

inspecting his sneakers   or making his dog sit still

on the step
                    tonight we see Miguel walking Churro

down near Second Avenue   *This is stupid* Marta says

We should all be friends
                    Why? I say

He never even apologized to Dario   In fact I add   *he acts like*

it never even happened   That's not true says Marta

He still feels bad   You can see it from here   we all stop

and stare toward the corner

                    Look at his shoulders

Marta points   *All slumped and sad   I mean* Clarissa adds

Dario's not even mad anymore   we all turn toward Dario

Right? Marta asks
                         Nah Dario says *I don't really care*

I mean, people are always beating on me anyway

Wait I say   *That's not a reason   That doesn't make it okay!*

I mean, you can't choose your brother   but you can choose

your friends
                    Yeah says Dario   *but I don't want this to end up*

on me   I mean, how do you feel, Alma?   You were the one

in a thing with him
                         I pause for a second

That's a good question I think   then turning I take a deep breath

and head toward the corner   *Oh, snap* I hear Marta call out

Shush I wave my hand   fixing my gaze on Miguel

while Churro laps   at a leaking fire hydrant   Miguel lifts

his head long before I reach him   just stands staring as

I approach   perspiration mists my lip   as it hits me

that I have no idea what I'm going to say   I shake off

Grandma Miriam's voice in my head   chiding *Fools rush in* and focus on the word *apology*

                    You need to apologize!

I announce too soon   *What's that?* Miguel asks   taking

a couple of steps to meet me   *I said you need to apologize to*

Dario   if you want to hang out with us again   And you

need to stop making fun of gay people   and just be

their friends   And you can't go around punching people

just because you feel mad   because that's a red flag

and I can never be your girl   but maybe we can all

be friends   as long as you promise   to never do any

of that again!

                I pause and place my hands on my hips

in a way that means   *I'm waiting*   *Well?* I say   Miguel looks

ready to cry   *I'm sorry* he mumbles

                  Don't tell me I say

Tell Dario   *Okay* he says pulling Churro   *Let's go*

Fourteen

I turned fourteen   the day before   my mom took a plane

to San Francisco   we still had a festive celebration, though

I got a twenty-dollar bill   and new headphones   from

my grandparents   who acted like   my mother wasn't

going anywhere
                            plus a pile of books and some clothes

from my parents   I also got permission   to see the midnight

screening of *Poltergeist*   that evening at the St. Marks

Cinema
                    this year we had a big meal

at a restaurant in Chinatown   so Grandfather could walk

Great-grandmother slowly   from their house   because

who knows   how many more birthdays   she has left

to celebrate and also   she really loves chocolate cake

we didn't have dinner at our place   like we usually do

because our apartment   is a mess of bags and boxes

with my mom's stuff spread out   across the beds and couch

outfits laid out
                            like empty versions of her   in accidental

action poses   I imagine as poised   for a walk in Golden

Gate Park   across the Mission District   or through the alleys

of San Francisco's Chinatown

                                                    all places my mother

has promised I'll visit   when I get to where she is

three thousand miles across the country   three hours

back in time   *In time* she said   *you will see why*

this trip is important for me   when we hugged at the gate

to her plane   I could already feel the weight

                    of whatever it was

Poltergeist

Is a movie in which *"Steven Spielberg   crosses a frightening*

new threshold"   it's also the most terrifying film   I have

ever seen   about a little girl   who talks to spirits

through the static on her TV

                              all hell breaks loose

when she's sucked   into the actual television set

and they have to tie   a rope around her mom   so she

can go get her daughter   from inside the closet   which

is really a portal to the evil netherworld

                                 whose *"form*

is revealed"   whose *"focus is clear"*   and which is scary enough

to be called *"harrowing"*   which is how I felt   when it was done

all *harrowed* out   from screaming about   the creepy tiny lady

with the creepy tiny voice   and the clown who pops up

from under the brother's bed   and tries to strangle him

halfway through

                         Miguel turns to me and says

I'm never going to the circus again   *I know* I whisper wincing

a little   as Clarissa digs her nails   into my knee

How can you see? Dario laughs   as I shrink down in my seat

my fingers spread   like a fan over my eyes

I can see fine I say   but I can't stop seeing   the mom

with the rope around her waist

                              even at the end

when the dad pushes   the television set

out of their room   at the Holiday Inn

                    and the whole theater cracks up

Stardust Is Not a Candy

It's a miracle you still have teeth   Dario is teasing me

You should talk   I say fake-surprised   *You eat as much candy*

as I do
                    Nope, that's impossible he argues

No way I say   *You're the one with a brother*   *plus your mother*

leaves her change all over the house   *True* Dario nods

But every time I see you   he continues   *you're munching*

something   laughing he imitates me   smoothing my ponytail

ripping off a wrapper   gobbling noisily

                                        Something that

you *gave me!* I say   *True* Dario admits   *I like to share*

I'm nice like that he smiles   *But I never split my Snickers*

Right I nod   *Like how I'm always saving Starburst*

Not me Dario says   *Stardust sticks to my teeth*

Star-what? I ask

                    Stardust Dario repeats   *It sticks to my teeth*

Oh my god I laugh   *Is that what you call it?*   *Yeah, why?*

Dario asks genuinely puzzled   *It's Star*burst   *not Stardust*

I explain   enunciating each syllable   Dario shakes his head smiles sheepishly to himself   staring down at the pavement

I do this he says   *Do what?* I ask   *Mix up my* b*'s and* d*'s*

Read stuff wrong   Everybody does that

once in a while I offer

                                 Yeah, well   Dario sighs

I do it a lot   Like I called February   Fevruary until

I was nine   They used to think   I had problems with

my sight   But it's more a reading thing

                                        Hey I say

You know we're made of stardust, right?

Dario raises his eyebrows   *What do you mean?*

Well, my mom once told me   that everything in the world

comes from stars   that chemical reactions inside stars

scattered their dust across the universe

                                          Whoa

says Dario   *I know!* I say   *Like all the dirt and water*

on Earth   and elements like carbon and iron   contain

stardust

                       Okay says Dario   sounding skeptical

for a second   *What about cars and trash?   I mean,*

we made those

Yes I agree   *But without the stars*

there is no Earth   And without the Earth   we don't exist

And without us   there's no garbage or cars   Every single

thing on the planet   has stardust in it   It's just the way

it is

        That's crazy Dario mumbles rubbing his head

So I say   *you've been calling it Stardust   your whole life*

Dario shrugs *Pretty much   That's messed up* I say

But kind of beautiful

                Yeah Dario agrees

Okay I say   *Just to be clear*   I point at the air

Stardust is not *a candy   True* says Dario

More like a beautiful accident or something

July

I don't know if there's a word   for the wavy way

that haze rises up from asphalt   when the weather's

superhot for weeks on end

                                        if there isn't such a word

there should be   it would also have to mean   the feeling

that is July   when every night I fall asleep   under a thin

sheet and every morning wake up late   my neck stiff

from the fan blowing   directly on it for ten hours straight

each new day   another blank page   for me to fill

with hanging out   chores around the house   and baby-

sitting from time to time

                                        that word would also have

to describe   how afternoons spent at the pool

on our bikes or on a stoop   all run together   the way

we do   so that Monday could be Wednesday could be Friday

for all we know or care

                                        how I can only tell it's Sunday

because my dad isn't driving the cab   because he and I have

time to share bagels for breakfast   plus even a little coffee for me   instead of just having   dinner during the week

when all I want to do is leave   and go back out with my friends

This isn't a hotel my dad says   but smiling as he says it

adding a *Be careful out there*   *Don't lose your keys again*

I'll be up when you get in   always an *I love you, kid*

Letter to Maureen

July 10, 1982

Dear Maureen,

 I bet you've gotten your period by now. I bet you also get cramps like me. Plus, you also probably feel cranky and tired at times. My mom says that's perfectly normal, and is because of hormones—that we are changing a lot.
 I wonder if you celebrated the 4th of July. This year I went with my dad to my uncle Aaron's roof with a good view of the show over the river. I love the ones that look like exploding flowers— like the chrysanthemum tea my grandmother sometimes makes for me with tons of sugar.
 I also love the pool this year—colder than ever and with new blue paint that doesn't flake. It's not the same without you, though. Write back wherever you are.

Love, Alma

P.S. My mom is in San Francisco. I am going there to meet her.

Postcard from Mom

July 20, 1982

Dear Alma,

This is a photo of San Francisco's Lombard Street—famous for its hills and hairpin turns. I can't wait for you to see it in person. The weather here is gorgeous and their Chinatown is much bigger than ours—so many wonderful markets and restaurants. My friend Anne has a great place with a view of the bay and plenty of space for you to stay. I miss you a lot, sweetie. I called earlier this week, but Dad said you were out with your friends. I will try again. The time difference makes it tricky! Looking forward to showing you around.

Love always,
Mom

John F. Kennedy

Was the thirty-fifth president of the United States   it's also

the name of an airport in Queens, New York   where my dad

and I are waiting   at my gate   for an American Airlines

plane to take me away   to San Francisco

Okay, kiddo

my dad says   rubbing his hands together   pacing

the navy carpet   *Okay* I smile

You've got your Walkman

he says   *and your extra batteries   and your book*

Your ticket's right here   Is that everything?

Wait I ask   *what about my bag?   How will I get it once*

I'm there? my dad holds up a finger   *Right!*

There's a stewardess on the plane   who'll look out for you

She'll know what to do   and make sure you find Mom

and your bag when you land

Right I nod

First plane ride ever I add   *Hope we don't crash* my dad smiles

squeezes my hand   *You don't have to worry about that*

You're flying "the friendly skies"   I think that's United I say

Anyway, it looks like they opened the door

All right,

you're up! he claps   *Oh, and here*   my dad reaches into

the pocket of his jeans   *I almost forgot*   *I got you some gum*

It helps with the pressure in your ears   *And here* he says

handing me a twenty-dollar bill   *A little cash for walking*

around   *Thanks* I tuck the money in my carry-on

Oh, and here my dad adds   producing a small pack

of salted cashews   *Better than those lousy peanuts*

he winks   *I think you're going to have a great time*

Same here   I murmur into his shoulder   my eyes

shut tight   against nervous tears

Fear of Flying

I am glad that I don't have   a fear of flying   like the rabbi

seated next to me   I am also glad   that I don't have

fourteen cousins   like the trumpet player   to my right

Because cousins are always asking   for money like

you're made of it   which Leon isn't   even if he is

a working musician who once played   on *The Tonight Show*

Starring Johnny Carson

I am crunching my cashews

minding my own business   sandwiched between

Leon and Rabbi Isaac   who've been talking across me

as our plane waits   for what feels like forever

on the *tarmac*   a word I just heard Isaac use   to describe

the delays on dozens of flights   he's taken all over

the world

Isaac who's spent his seventy-two years living

in Flatbush, Brooklyn   not far from my grandma Miriam

who somehow he didn't know   but *Miriam Levin!*

Now, she was a rose   according to Isaac anyway

it's my *lucky day*   because Isaac hates to fly   and to pass

the time he talks   almost as much as Leon does   only

Leon discusses jazz musicians   such as Thelonious Monk

whose name I mistake   as *The Loneliest Monk*   which

makes Isaac and Leon laugh so hard   they actually slap

their knees   saying things like

Priceless!

and *Monk was no monk!*   which means nothing to me

but takes my mind off   the evacuation instructions

our stewardess is acting out   and which everyone

is ignoring   I don't want to think about our plane

flying over the ocean   or about using my seat as

a flotation device

so I call on some mental kung fu

to focus my mind   with a mantra about my mom

See you soon

See you soon

See you soon

I repeat   as we prepare for takeoff   I pop in some gum

put my headphones on   along with some Blondie

at thirty thousand feet   Leon nudges me   hands me

a cassette   with a label   that says *A Love Supreme*

in blue ballpoint pen   I've heard of that   *John Coltrane?* I ask

Leon nods   then tells me the story   of the song's creation

how like a lot of jazz   it was the product of spontaneous

chemistry
                    how Coltrane's religious faith fused

with his music   so that the whole piece   became a saxophone

ode to God   also how Coltrane wrote a poem   to go with it

because he was such a genius
                                        I tell Leon I don't think

I believe in God   but that I wrote a creation myth

about being born in a wok   in my mother's kitchen

Right on! Leon says   shaking his head   a gold-capped molar

peeking out   from behind his wide grin
                                        Right on!

Rabbi Isaac repeats   smoothing his beard as he leans over

and mouths *What are we talking about?*   *Coltrane* says Leon

I saw him play! Isaac shouts   *You don't say?* whispers Leon

in a way that kind of implies   Rabbi Isaac is shouting

At the Village Vanguard in 1962   Isaac continues   *I had no idea who Coltrane was   or who he was going to become*

Yeah Leon laughs   *We're all trying to become someone,*

I guess   Until we are   then turning to me   Leon asks

And what are you doing on this plane by yourself?

I'm going to see my mom I explain

                                      Your parents divorced?

I nod and squash   a small bubble of gum   between

my teeth and my tongue   so that it snaps   like punctuation

Getting I say

                    That's an unfortunate situation Leon replies

Yes I agree   *But it's okay*

I don't have to move or anything

Really? Isaac interrupts   *When my son got divorced*

his wife took their kids to Florida   Can you imagine?

Leaving Brooklyn to go there?

                           Well, it's warm I offer

Yes Rabbi Isaac nods *But the food*   *Yeah* adds Leon

I played Miami once   But Miami's got that good Cuban cuisine

at least   Even so Isaac shakes his head   *I don't like having*

my grandchildren so far away

Yeah Leon says

My kids are down south   with their mother and her cousins

I get there for a week   every couple of months   It works out

all right   I might move down there sometime   Maybe near

New Orleans
                    Well I explain

My mom is just visiting her friend   Then she's coming

home again   I'm starting high school
                                                High school?

Right on! says Leon   *Right on* I smile

when the cabin lights go dim   everyone settles in

gets quiet for a while   I take out the copy

of *The Catcher in the Rye*   my dad gave me for the ride

and press Play on *A Love Supreme*
                                        its opening notes

which sound like a tender ache   mixed with rain

make me want to cry   all of a sudden   I don't know why

because I don't feel sad   and I'm not afraid to fly   but

as Isaac to my left softly snores   and Leon to my right

drums his thighs   I feel like life   like this plane

like really everything   could veer in any direction

at any moment   the whole thing   so alive and open

                          it's almost hard to take

Sunbirds

You're here! my mom claps   as I step off the escalator

and rush toward her   *I'm sooo tired* I say   while she

crushes me in a hug   smells my hair   smooths

my ponytail   takes a good long look at my face

You have your period she smiles

                                        Yeah, why? I sigh

I can see it in your eyes   A little dreamy   Come

she takes my bag   kisses my hand   and leads me

through a set of giant glass doors   to where her friend

Anne is waiting   by the curb   leaning against her car

a Sunbird   just like my cousin's   but white with black

fuzzy dice hanging   from the rearview mirror

Cool car I say   *My cousin J had one like this   Oh, yeah?*

Anne says extending her hand   I meet hers with mine

and she pulls me in   for a quick embrace   *Alma!*

I've heard so much about you!   Me too I respond

even though it's not really true

                                        I don't know

much about Anne   except that she and Mom

were college friends   here in California   that when

they talk long-distance on the phone   it's expensive

and they laugh really hard   that my mom has been

wanting to visit Anne   ever since I was born

                                                                within

twenty minutes   we're speeding across

the Golden Gate Bridge   and over San Francisco Bay

It's all so beautiful!   I say half gasping *Wow*   while

the wind whips my ponytail   through the open window

Let's go straight to Chinatown!   my mom calls out

There's a great dumpling house   I want you to try

above us   the sky is a swirl of clouds   tinged with orange

and peach like a Creamsicle

                                          I am tired but I feel energized

and my mom seems alive   in a way that's new   *Tomorrow*

can we go to the zoo? I shout   gulping gusts of air

We can go anywhere we want   my mom replies

Like Sunbirds I say   smiling through a yawn

Postcard to Dad

August 8, 1982

Dear Dad,

    This is a picture of Lombard Street. It's very famous because it's so steep and has a lot of hairpin turns. Mom and I walked up and down it with Anne until our legs were wobbly. We also went to the zoo, where we saw the most beautiful lions. When the male lion roared, the sound was so deep I could feel it in my bones. Also, the Chinatown here is so much bigger than the one at home and they have excellent dumplings!

    I miss you. Mom says I can call you on Sunday night when the rates are low.

Love, Alma

P.S. Mom says hello.

Postcard to Clarissa, Dario, and Miguel

August 8, 1982

Dear Clarissa, Dario, and Miguel,

    This is a picture of Lombard Street. It's very famous because it's so steep and has a lot of hairpin turns. My mom and I walked up and down it with her friend Anne until our legs were wobbly. We also went to the zoo, where we saw the most beautiful lions. When the male lion roared, the sound was so deep I could feel it in my bones. Also, I ate excellent dumplings in Chinatown, which is much bigger than the one at home.

    I miss you guys. Mom says I can't call any of you on the phone. Too expensive!

Love, Alma

P.S. DO NOT see <u>Blade Runner</u> without me!

North Beach

Is the neighborhood   where Anne lives   in a small blue house

on a hill   which means every day   we can walk to the wharf

and buy fresh fish   for my mom to fry up   in a pan with

scallions and ginger   which we eat over rice   each night

while watching the sun   reflect off the bay
                                        today my mom

and I are taking a break   from seeing the sights   to drink tea

play with Anne's cat   read books and draw   and talk

about life
                it's funny to hear Anne tell stories

about my mom as a college student   a young woman

from even before she met my dad   when Mom and Anne

reminisce   there's something   in their voices

that catches   reminds me of Ms. Nola
                                        how once

she shook her head in disbelief   about a poster

in her office being so old   something about how *time flies*

even though she didn't   say those actual words   I could

hear the feeling   can hear a similar sense   in my mom's

laugh

        more forceful and open than usual

can see it   in how the sunshine   coming through

the window   makes her look more beautiful   as she

remembers a time   she and Anne went to Big Sur

and lost the keys to her car   in the surf

Golden Gate Bridge

A *wonder of the modern world*   the Golden Gate Bridge

spans the strait that connects   San Francisco Bay

to the Pacific Ocean   massive and gorgeous and orange

the exact word for its color   is *vermilion*   which must

also mean bold
                        which is how I feel

walking its length   with my mom   our hands clasped

and swinging lightly   in time with our steps   each

of us lifting the other's arm   every now and again

to point out   features of the incredible view   sky-

scrapers in the distance   hills dotted with houses

It's easy to forget   to look up my mom says   yanking

our arms skyward   toward a bank of clouds   almost

close enough to touch
                         It's hard not to look everywhere

I say   making a sweeping gesture   across the water

with our hands   when the wind kicks up   tossing our hair

around our faces   so that it tangles up   like a single mane we laugh and shriek   because we can hardly see   I'm

wearing my hair loose   for the first time   since I was nine

it was Anne's idea   the other night   to brush it through

with special oil   so we could see how much   it looks like

my mother's   how much I look like her

                                           but also how different

Dumplings

My mom and I   are eating dumplings again   this time

at a tiny parlor on Old Chinatown Lane   while Anne takes

her cat to the vet
               So my mom says

how are you liking San Francisco?   *I love it* I say

It's like heaven   *Mmmm* my mom nods   slurping soup broth

into her mouth   from a wide porcelain spoon   *Oops*

she smiles   wiping her chin with a napkin

These dumplings are superjuicy   I laugh   *They really are*

she replies   reaching for another
                   So she says again

Is this a place   *you could imagine living in?*   *Sure* I shrug

Like what? When I grow up?   *Well* my mom answers

dipping her dumpling   into a dish of chili oil

Like now she says   staring straight into my face   as if

she's searching   for a response   before I even have one

But we live in New York I sigh   half rolling my eyes   *I mean,*

maybe one day   *Well* my mom says again   *I was thinking maybe we could live here now   I mean, move out here*

for a while   What? I laugh   *And live with Anne?*

No, not with Anne   but maybe near her in North Beach

There are some houses for lease   not far from where she is

Wait, what? I fumble my chopsticks   accidentally flipping

one onto the floor   *We live in New York* I say   *That's where*

we're from   That's where we live with Dad   Or did

but still

That's our home

                         You know, Alma my mom begins

I've lived in places other than New York   People sometimes move

if they want to be somewhere new   Well, I don't want to be

somewhere new I insist   *I want to live with you and Dad*

In New York   my voice is trembling   so that when

the waiter brings me   a fresh set of chopsticks   I can

barely croak a quick *Thank you*   before asking for

more water   before the tears   begin to pour down

my cheeks and into my soup   as I reach to smooth

my ponytail   I remember that my hair is loose   which

all of a sudden   is exactly how I feel

                              undone

Undone

Some things can't be undone   like when someone sets

her mind to something   sometimes there's nothing

that can be done to change it

      some things   someone   sometimes   my mom

is as stubborn   as she says I am   like now   how she wants

to convince me   to start a new life with her   here

in San Francisco   a beautiful place   that is not my home

filled with people   who are not my people   except for

maybe Anne   and really only *maybe*   since she's the only

other person I know   and the kind of *people*   I am

talking about   are the kind that take time   time I don't have

before I leave   at the end of the week   to fly home

to New York

       I'm finding it hard to speak

with my mom   about this issue   without crying

angry tears   without fear of a future   far from

my friends   and away from my dad   filling my mind

clouding my vision like smoke   so that I can only

shake my head

                    choke *No*

as in *I'm not coming back here*   while my mom and Anne

try in their way   to give me space   to think to sleep

to talk on the phone with my dad   about how sad I feel

about divorce   how mad I am   about being given a *choice*

that puts me between   *a rock and a hard place*

                                        which is what

Grandma Miriam would say   if she were here   but she is not

it's just my mom   who is everything to me   and not

everything to me   plus all the spaces in between

Mystery: Long Distance

Okay I rasp   *I'll make it fast*   *I know long distance*

is expensive   plus it's not even Sunday so—

Don't worry

about that, kiddo my dad says   sounding sort of tired

Oh jeez, Dad   I forgot it's like one a.m. in New York

the time difference   reminding me of just how   far away

my real life is

Your mom   my dad is saying

has always loved California   has always wanted

to move there   Well, that's news to me I snort

Look my dad sighs   *I support you   Whatever*

you choose to do

Wait I ask

did you know Mom wanted to move?   Yes says my dad

clearing his throat   *We spoke about it   before she left*

And you're okay with that? I ask   *Okay with it?* my dad repeats

pausing he adds   *Your mother is a grown woman*

She has to do what's best for her   What about me?

I want to know

She thinks San Francisco

would be wonderful for you   Well, what do you think?

I think . . .   my dad stops for a second   in the silence

of a couple of breaths   I can hear him measure his words

I think we are a family   No amount of distance will

change that
                      That   I insist   *is ridiculous*

How can our family not be changed   if we are living

so far away?
                      You're right my dad agrees

How about changed but not broken?   Like in your mental

kung fu?   Okay I say   *How about I stay a New Yorker*

and still live with you?
                      Okay says my dad

But how about you take   more time to decide?

You can always change your mind

Your mind is yours to change
                      Okay I say

Should I Stay or Should I Go?

This indecision's bugging me (Esta indecisión me molesta)
If you don't want me, set me free (Si no me quieres, librarme)
Exactly whom I'm supposed to be (Dígame que tengo ser)
Don't you know which clothes even fit me? (Sabes qué ropa
me quedrá)

          —The Clash, "Should I Stay or Should I Go"

I am listening   to "Should I Stay or Should I Go"

on my Walkman   while my mom and Anne mill

around the kitchen   frying fish and singing along

to the Beatles
              it's not lost on me

that this song by the Clash   is extremely literal in how

its lyrics describe the dilemma   I am facing

in fact that's exactly   why I am listening to it

because even though I used to tease Miguel   for being

really literal   it's a relief to hear   Joe Strummer howl

and pluck his guitar   while Topper Headon smashes

his drum kit to bits   as they repeat the very question

I've had in my head   for three days

I'm also listening

for extra advice   from the Spanish in the song   as if another

language   will reveal some insight   I don't have but need

before I leave San Francisco   on a flight

back home

where I can stay or I can go   depending

Phoenix

parable :
a usually short fictitious story that illustrates
a moral attitude or a religious principle

My mother likes   to speak in parables sometimes

meaning she'll tell me   a random story about life

then leave it to me   to figure out the point   which is irritating

especially if Anne is around   nodding her head   as she

waters her plants   as if she understands this thing

between my mom and me   which she really doesn't get at all

The phoenix   my mom begins   completely out of nowhere

as if we had been talking   about birds this whole time

is a regal bird   *Yeah, I know about the phoenix* I say

I learned about that last year

                      Well, the Chinese phoenix

she continues *is different from the Greeks'*   *Fenghuang rules*

over all the birds in the world   *and holds sacred scrolls*

in his talons   *He comes from the sun*   *is a symbol of harmony*

between opposites   *like the yin and yang*   *male and female hot and cold and so on*

                                   So? I sigh   nodding vaguely

at Anne   who's smiling and holding up   the black-and-white

yin-yang ornament   that hangs in her window

I roll my eyes   without really meaning to   try to cover it

with a smile

                        meanwhile my mom

is still going on about how the phoenix   lives in the mountains

how its feet are symbols of the Earth   its head, the sky

You know I say   *I heard there's a Phoenix constellation*

but that in China   *you can only see the whole thing*   *from*

certain parts of the country   *since it's only made of four stars*

and China is so vast

                      Really? Wow! Anne exclaims

in a tone you'd use with a five-year-old   I resist rolling my eyes

this time   but I'm rolling them inside   also cursing her

intrusiveness and her silly hippie-speak   how Anne's always

saying *Far out!*

                meanwhile my mom's trying

to bring the exchange back   to how *the presence*

of the phoenix   *is a sign of peace and happiness*

I turn toward the window   grab my Walkman

and pop in a cassette
                                    Well I say snapping

shut the deck   and pulling my headphones on

                    Definitely no phoenixes here

The Spaces in Between

Is what I would call   the dream I had last night   if I had

to give it a name

in the dream

I am alone in Anne's blue house   sitting cross-legged

on her purple couch   listening to records

from a collection   she keeps stacked in wooden

apple crates along the wall

it's late at night

I have the idea to call Ms. Nola   but can't remember

where I put her number   so I put on an album instead

Rumours by Fleetwood Mac   which has a man

with a ponytail on its cover   and a woman twirling

a silky scarf   the whole scene   looks kind of lame

but the music is pretty decent   all the same

especially a song called   "Go Your Own Way"

in the dream   I find a letter addressed to me   inside

the wrinkled album sleeve   what Ms. Foster would call

a *recurring motif*   but whatever

it's written on a thin

strip of paper   like the kind   you'd find in a fortune cookie

and it says:

> Dear Alma,
> The spaces in between the vinyl grooves
> are where you'll find the truth.
> Listen hard.

but all I can decipher is the line   *You can go your own way*

which isn't a mysterious thing to say   not the kind of statement

you'd need a dream to make

if like my dad says

Dreams are the heart's way   of talking to the mind

in a manner that the self can deal with

this morning

I stayed a long time in bed   cuddling with Anne's cat

trying to understand   what the dream meant

Sassafras   I whispered in his ear   *I think it means*

I can handle this

Long Distance

I am pretty sure   I am not supposed to be calling

long-distance   unless it's my dad   but my mom and Anne

are still asleep in their beds   and I've been thinking a lot

about Ms. Nola since my dream

                                        as I dial the first digits

of her number   on Anne's purple princess phone   it's as if

my finger can remember   the feeling of calling Grandma

Miriam back in Brooklyn   Sunday evenings after my bath

before I'd go to bed   when all sprawled out   on the rug

in my pajamas   I'd look at a book   while she and I talked

about I don't know what   whatever a little kid   like me

had on her mind at the time   knock-knock jokes

or cartoons   or how much we'd weigh   on the moon

as soon as my call to Ms. Nola connects   and her line

begins to ring   my heart starts beating quickly   I carry

the phone   from the kitchen to the hallway   for privacy

even though everyone is asleep   I'm mouthing

Stop, Sassafras at Anne's cat who's batting the cord

with his paw
                    Ms. Nola finally picks up

with a drowsy *Hello* *Shoot!* I think then speak

Hi, Ms. Nola I say *It's me, Alma* *I'm sorry I'm calling*

in the middle of the night *I forgot about the time*

Alma? Ms. Nola repeats *Yes* I say *Alma Rosen*

Hi, honey, I know says Ms. Nola *Everything all right?*

Sure I respond *I just wanted to call and say hello*

before I go to high school *I'm in San Francisco right now*

with my mom
                    Um, okay Ms. Nola says sounding

a little perplexed *It's August, so there's still time left*

Yeah I laugh awkwardly *I also wanted to tell you about*

this book *I found at my mom's friend Anne's house*

Okay Ms. Nola replies
                    It's by that Ram Dass guy

It's called Be Here Now *Yes* Ms. Nola says a little more awake

I read that a long time ago *Have you?* *No* I reply

But the cover says *it's about meditation* *which might have*

to do with mental kung fu   so I thought you might be

interested

                    Okay, honey Ms. Nola says

I can hear her sitting up   *What else is going on?*

Well I add   *I also found this record by George Harrison*

He was one of the Beatles

                              Yes Ms. Nola says

I know who he is   And I continue   *there's this song on it*

called "Be Here Now"   George Harrison wrote it   because

he also really likes Ram Dass   It goes "Remember now,

be here now   As it's not like it was before"

                                        Wow

Ms. Nola says   sounding genuinely amazed   *That's quite*

a connection you've made   What's that all about?

Um I pause for a moment   to consider her question

I'm not sure   It just seemed deep to me   so I wanted

to tell you about it

                    Well, I'm glad you did, Alma

Ms. Nola answers   with a smile I can hear

Are you looking forward to next year?

                              Yes I say

Pretty much   Anything else you want to discuss?   she wants

to know   *Nothing really* I reply   *I just wanted to say hi*

Well, hello, Ms. Alma   I'm very glad you called

Same here I say   before hanging up   *Thank you so much*

Letter to Persephone

Dear Persephone,

I'm between a rock and a hard place, as my grandma Miriam would say. And it's a tough space to be in. I hope you're not stuck in the underworld right now. I am thinking of you—wondering what you would advise me to do.

I can't write to my grandma Miriam, because she passed away, or to my friends, because it would take too long for them to respond. I can't call them either, since it costs too much and they're hardly ever home anyway. Faith is the only one who has an answering machine, but she's in Nantucket. Which we call Nah—fuck—it. Which is sometimes how I feel. Which is how I think you might feel sometimes too.

Love, Alma

Undone

Some things   can't be undone   like a person

because a person   is not a bed   or a head of hair

because a person is always   in the process of becoming

       some things   someone   sometimes

I think you can decide   to unravel

or to gather yourself up   sometimes

it's enough   just to go your own way

Home

It's a sunny day   I'm standing   at the counter in Ray's

pointing at the plexiglass case   with a fistful of change

the bells ring and Marta walks in

Oh, snap! she shouts

You're back!   and throws her arms   around my shoulders

Oh, snap is right! I laugh   our hug releasing Marta's familiar

scent of cocoa butter   one of her tiny gold hoops   a quick

spot of warmth   against my cheek

You were gone for two

whole weeks she says   *I know* I reply   *I was with my mom*

and her friend   We got the postcard you sent   Marta adds

San Francisco looks so cool   Yeah I nod   *It's really beautiful*

Maybe I'll live there someday I say

Really? Marta raises

her eyebrows   *Yes* I nod again   *My mom is actually going*

to move there for a while   But I think I'm staying here

Wow, okay Marta slows down   *Sounds like we need to talk*

I nod as my eyes well up   *C'mon, we'll hang on my roof*

And no offense she adds   *but your hair is a mess*

                                           I know

I laugh *I have jet lag*   *plus I just woke up*   *Well* Marta says

I've got my brush   *Let's go up and untangle this stuff*

Stuff

Marta takes a hank of my hair in her fist   *This is the worst*

I've ever seen it   she mumbles   under her breath

raking the brush across my head   and down a length

of hair   *Ow!* I squeal   *Not so hard!*

                                     I haven't even started

she laughs   *You should really put some oil*   *on this mess*

I'm not sure I can deal with it   Marta sighs   puts her brush

on the towel   we've spread out on the tar rooftop   turning

to face me she says   *San Francisco is far, you know*

                                     Believe me

I nod *I know*   *I mean, my mom's not even home*

She's in California   So Marta opens her hands   *What?*

Is she just going to move there?   *Yep* I nod

Aren't you scared   *you'll never see her again?* Marta asks

Like Maureen?   *Yes and no*   *I mean, it's my mom*   *But still,*

she helps me with everything   *But I'm also old enough to do*

things on my own, so . . .

                        That's true Marta agrees

Like if you were a baby   *this would be terrible*   *But* I continue *it doesn't feel like home   when my mom's not there   even her*

clothes and stuff   her waking me up   That's true too

Marta nods   *Plus, your dad can't cook   I know* I add

That's what my mom always says   But he's been trying

He got a book
                    Ay dios mío, Alma Marta sighs

What are you going to do?   Your mom will be sad if you stay

And your dad will be sad if you go   And then there's me

and Clarissa and Faith   And Dario and Miguel and Churro

Churro? I laugh
                    Yeah, you're right   He doesn't care

But you know what I mean   Our whole crew would feel

different without you   Everything is changing I say

Do you feel that way? I ask   turning to look at Marta

from over my shoulder
                    Yes she says

But there's nothing we can do   Except, I guess, what we want

I suggest   we sit in silence for a couple of seconds   before

I start speaking again   *I mean, my mom's always wanted*

to move back to California   How come I never knew that?

I ask   my voice cracking slightly   as I say it

You're telling me   Marta shakes her head

There's a lot we don't know   *I found out last year*

that my mom was in love   *with this guy before my dad*

What's so bad about that? I ask   *A lot of people fall in love*

before they meet each other

                              Yeah Marta continues

But he was married   *Oh, okay* I nod   *That's not good*

Yeah she agrees   *And then she met my dad*   *and went with him*

because she was mad or something   *That's how she got*

my brother

                Wow I say   *Is that the reason*

they stayed together?   *Well* Marta explains   *not exactly*

But eventually   *It's complicated*

                                    Sure is I agree

slipping my hair into a ponytail   with an elastic

from my wrist   *This is good* I add   *What is?* Marta asks

Talking I respond   Marta hesitates for a moment

then says   *So, what are you going to do?*

                                    I don't know

I shrug   *My dad says I should take my time*   *that I can*

always change my mind
                    Your dad's a good guy says Marta

I know I reply   *And your mom is cool too* Marta continues

Yeah, but together I explain   *they just don't work*

It's like they're cursed   to love each other but never get along

Marta shakes her head   *Like in a bad song*
                              Exactly I laugh

I mean, San Francisco is really nice   But I don't want a whole

new life   I want my old life   the one where my grandma

Miriam is alive   and I'm five and everyone gets along just fine

So do I Marta says   stretching out on her towel   *I loved living*

in Puerto Rico when I was little   And you know how much

Miguel misses Cuba? No I answer   *A lot* adds Marta

It's not fair that everything has to change I say   gazing past

the potted plants and laundry lines   dotting the roofs

of the Lower East Side   *I think even grown-ups feel*

this way sometimes
                    I put my hand at my brow

like a visor   to shield my face   from the white-hot sun

burning through the clouds   over Second Avenue

the noon light almost blinding   against the bright

blue sky

         when I shut my eyes

I can feel sweat tingle   on the back of my neck

as my ponytail brushes my skin

                  from behind my closed lids

I see a fiery rush   of orange and vermilion blossoms

flickering like a Super 8 movie   like the filmstrips

I watched as a kid

           everything shifting and changing

           lit from within

Rise and Shine

I'm scrambling eggs and lox   in my mother's wok

which I love cooking in   for the way the blue flames   flicker

and lick the curved sides   of the cast iron seasoned

by years of fat   salt and soy sauce

                        I hear my mom's

chopsticks clicking in my mind   I see her sliding

a whole fish into a bath of bubbling oil   fragrant

with finely minced ginger   she'd chopped with her giant

cleaver

        but she's not here

and my dad's out   food shopping for the week

the apartment feels strange   with just me   and so many

spaces still holding   my mother's absence

                        from the place

she'd hang her apron   now draped like a crumpled shadow to

the spot on the shelf by the stove   where she would prop her

book   if a casserole was baking   and she could find

a few minutes to read

                standing in front of the oven

I remember   how my mother taught me   to light its flame

how she prompted me   to teach myself

                                        by handing me

the matches and leaving the kitchen   her meaning was clear

Your fear is in your mind   Time to let go

                                        in that moment

my mom let me know   I was growing   that I'd grown

like how she used to say   when I was little   I'd sometimes

wake from a nap   with my head looking bigger

or my features slightly different

                            how running

in the playground   I swear there were times   I could feel

my bones getting longer   getting stronger   as I chased

a ball across the asphalt

                        how now

as I stir eggs gently   over low heat   I hesitate to choose

between people and places I love   but know that I can

                            that I must

Up on the Roof

On the roof, it's peaceful as can be
And there the world below can't bother me

    —The Drifters, "Up on the Roof"

Miguel is crooning a cappella   snapping his fingers

and nodding his head   *How do you even know that song?*

Dario wants to know   *It sounds so old and corny*

I know, man says Miguel   *I don't know   My parents have*

these records they brought from Cuba   I used to listen

to them when I was little
                              Whatever says Dario

It sounds wack   like doo-wop   Okay, enough Clarissa cuts in

waving a copy of the *New York Post   Are we going to the movies*

tonight or what?   Yes! everyone shouts at once   *Okay, then*

she huffs   *Blade Runner, 6:45, St. Marks   Great* says Dario

Why do you sound like our mother? laughs Miguel
                                                   Wait!

I jump up   *It's Sunday, right?   Yup* Dario replies

Okay, then I say turning   *Wait for me   I'll be back*

Long Distance

You know you didn't have to wait   *until the rates were low*

my dad says   when I come home and tell him   *I know* I say

I just needed a few more days

                                        Okay he nods *You sure?*

You know you can always—   *I know* I interrupt   *All right* he says

handing me the phone   before going into the kitchen   so I can

have some privacy

                        I dial and wait

for the call to go through   picturing a swirl of numbers

the 4 the 1 the 5   traveling along wires   deep beneath

the ocean   that separates our coasts   East and West

and all the spaces in between   on the fifth ring

my mother picks up

                        Hi, Mom I say   *It's me, Alma*

Free

I don't know why   I feel so free sometimes   speeding

down the street   on my banana seat   the white tassels

on my handlebars   splayed like feathers   in the wind

this doesn't happen most days   but when it does   I could

cruise around   my neighborhood for hours   my places

and my people   just a blur   as I circle Tompkins Square

or St. Mark's Church   my hair whipping behind me

free to be me   going anywhere   I want to be

RECOGNIZE

Gratitude to my husband, Pete, and our three children—Cormac, Alma, and Titian—for being my earliest readers, and for their support and encouragement during the making of this book. Special thanks to *my* Alma, who was the very first person to read the very first draft and whose insightful suggestions were a big help.

Eternal thanks to Christopher Myers for having the vision to propose that this book was indeed possible, and for being such a supportive creative force along the way. Deep appreciation for Michelle Frey's and Arely Guzmán's enthusiasm and hard work in bringing this book into the world, and to the team of copy editors and designers for their eagle eyes and amazing attention to detail.

Shout-out, too, to poet Matthew Lippman, who—bighearted reader—really made me feel like I had something here, and who also offered valuable practical advice. Old-school props to Dave Arons for reading an initial version, for believing that my stories were worth telling, and for always being such a steadfast friend. Appreciation to Jacqueline Woodson for being so open, for assuring me "You've got this," and for chiming in with cherished encouragement. And thanks also to every kid I ever taught or knew, every friend, and every crew. You're all in here. How could you not be? I've learned from each of you. We really do *contain multitudes*.

NOTES

p. 47: In the poem "On Our Block," I mention a play called *My Son the Waiter: A Jewish Tragedy,* which, written by Brad Zimmerman in 2014, is not contemporaneous with most other references in this book. It's just such a timeless, hilarious characterization, I had to use it here.

p. 242–243: In the poem "Creation Myth," I owe a debt to friend and poet Gregory Pardlo, whose poem "Written by Himself" (*Digest,* Four Way Books, 2014) served as inspiration for Alma's own homework-poem response. Look his up. It's great.

SONG PERMISSIONS